"We really don't have much in common." Nothing other than a baby, of course.

"I'll admit that it might look that way on the surface. But we don't know that for sure. We never really had a chance to talk much that night."

Shane was right about that. Even though they'd known each other's bodies intimately, the rugged cowboy was pretty much a stranger to Jillian—as she was to him.

But he'd also put her healing process on the fast track and had made her feel desirable again.

So did that make them friendly strangers?

Or strangers with benefits…?

Dear Reader,

Welcome back to Brighton Valley, where we'll move from summer to winter with Shane Hollister, a police detective turned cowboy, and Jillian Wilkes, who's pregnant with the cowboy's baby.

You'll get a chance to revisit Caroline's Diner, which has been adorned with a Christmas tree and all the trimmings. You'll also have a chance to catch up with Dan and Eva Walker, hero and heroine of *His, Hers and...Theirs?* as well as their two sets of twins. The youngest girls are toddlers now.

There's something special about a small Texas town during the holidays, especially when love is in the air. So find a cozy spot to curl up and read Shane and Jillian's story in *A Baby Under the Tree.*

Wishing you and yours a Merry Christmas and a happy new year,

Judy

A BABY UNDER THE TREE

JUDY DUARTE

Harlequin®

SPECIAL EDITION

Recycling programs
for this product may
not exist in your area.

ISBN-13: 978-0-373-65640-0

A BABY UNDER THE TREE

Other titles by Judy Duarte available in ebook

JUDY DUARTE

always knew there was a book inside her, but since English was her least-favorite subject in school, she never considered herself a writer. An avid reader who enjoys a happy ending, Judy couldn't shake the dream of creating a book of her own.

Her dream became a reality in March of 2002, when Silhouette Special Edition released her first book, *Cowboy Courage*. Since then, she has published more than twenty novels.

Her stories have touched the hearts of readers around the world. And in July of 2005, Judy won a prestigious Readers' Choice Award for *The Rich Man's Son*.

Judy makes her home near the beach in Southern California. When she's not cooped up in her writing cave, she's spending time with her somewhat enormous but delightfully close family.

To Susan Litman.
If they had an editor of the year award, you'd get my
nomination, my vote and my wholehearted applause.

Chapter One

As Jillian Wilkes entered El Jardin, an upscale bar in downtown Houston, she couldn't decide whether this was the most therapeutic move she'd ever made—or the craziest.

After all, how many thirty-year-old women celebrated the day their divorce was final when they'd gone from princess to pauper in a matter of months?

Not many, she supposed, unless they, too, had been humiliated by their wealthy husband's serial infidelity.

Eight years ago, marrying Thomas Wilkes had been a fairy-tale dream come true, but the split, which had created quite a stir in the highest social circles, had been a nightmare.

Now that the worst was behind her, she planned to treat herself to one last bit of fine dining and some much-needed pampering at a good spa before retreating to the real world in which she'd been born and raised.

So after leaving her lawyer's office, she'd checked in for the weekend at a nice but affordable hotel, then took a short walk to one of the newest and classiest bars in town. There she intended to raise a glass to salute her new life. No more grieving the past for her. Instead, she would embrace whatever changes the future would bring.

Now, as Jillian scanned the interior, with its white plaster walls adorned with lush, colorful hanging plants and an old-world-style fountain in the center of the room, she was glad she'd come.

She spotted an empty table at the back of the room, near a stone fireplace that had a gas flame roasting artificial logs. After crossing the Spanish-tiled floor, she pulled out a chair, took a seat and placed her black Coach purse at her feet.

For a moment, she considered her decision to make a good-riddance toast to Thomas Wilkes. Another woman might have just gone home to lick her wounds, but Jillian couldn't do that. Thanks to an ironclad prenuptial agreement—and the fact that all of the properties in which they'd ever lived during their marriage had been owned by the Wilkes family trust—Jillian didn't have a home to go to. But she'd remedy that on Monday, when she would find a modest, one-bedroom apartment near the university where she would start graduate school in the summer.

It was a good game plan, she decided, and one deserving a proper kickoff. She was a free woman. So out with the old, and in with the new.

As if on cue, a waiter stopped by the table and set a sterling silver bowl of mixed nuts in front of her. "Can I get you something to drink?"

"Yes, I'd like a split of the best champagne you have."

He nodded, then left to get her order. Minutes later, he returned with a crystal flute, a silver bucket of ice and a small bottle of Cristal.

The sound of the popping cork gave Jillian an unexpected lift.

"Shall I?" the waiter asked.

"Yes, please."

When he'd poured the proper amount, Jillian lifted her flute, taking a moment to watch the bubbles rise to the surface. Then she tapped the crystal glass against the bottle, setting off an elegant sound that promised better days ahead.

As she leaned back in her chair and took a sip of champagne, she surveyed the rest of the happy-hour crowd.

A forty-something man sat to her right, drinking something that appeared to be Scotch. She surmised he was a businessman because of the gray suit he was wearing—or rather, make that *had been* wearing. The jacket, which he'd probably hung on the back of his chair, had slipped to the floor.

When he glanced up, his eyes red and glassy, his tie loosened to the point of being sloppy, she realized he'd had a few drinks too many.

As their gazes met, he smiled and lifted his glass. "Hey, there, pretty lady. How 'bout I buy you a drink?"

She looked away, letting her body language tell him that she wasn't the least bit interested in having a bar-room buddy.

Maybe coming here hadn't been such a great idea, after all. She probably ought to pay her tab and head back to the hotel, where she could kick back, order room service and watch a pay-per-view movie.

That sounded a lot better than avoiding glances from an amorous drunk.

But before she could motion for the waiter, she spotted a dark-haired cowboy seated at a table near a potted palm tree, a worn Stetson resting on the chair beside him, his long denim-clad legs stretched out, revealing scuffed boots. His hair, which was in need of a trim, was a bit mussed, as though he'd run his hands through it a time or two.

Funny, but she hadn't noticed him before, which was odd. She wasn't sure how she could have missed seeing someone so intriguing, so out of place.

Who was he? And why had he chosen to stop off at El Jardin for a drink? Maybe it was the relaxed pose of his lean body and the way he gripped the longneck bottle, but it seemed to her that he'd be more comfortable in a sports bar or honky-tonk.

She had no idea how long she'd been studying him— longer than was polite, to be sure. So when he glanced up and noticed her interest in him, her cheeks flushed. She should have turned away, embarrassed to have been caught gawking at him, but the intensity of his gaze—

the heat of it—nearly knocked the breath and the good sense right out of her.

Unprepared for the visual connection or for her reaction to it, she finally broke eye contact by reaching into the silver bowl of nuts.

Three almonds and several sips of champagne later, she found herself turning her head once again—and catching him looking at her as though he'd never stopped.

A surge of sexual awareness shot through her, which didn't make a bit of sense.

How in the world could her first post-divorce interest in another man be directed at a *cowboy?* Goodness, Jillian had to be the only woman in Houston who didn't even like country music.

She tried to chalk it up to curiosity. Or to the fact that he couldn't be any less like her ex than if she'd joined an online dating service and specifically ordered someone brand-new.

When she turned her head and saw him still studying her intently, she realized that the interest was mutual. She might have been married for the past eight years, but she still remembered the kind of eye contact that went on between a man and woman who were attracted to each other.

Not that the cowboy was flirting with her. Or that she'd even flirt back.

If she were a free spirit, she might have asked him to join her. But that was even crazier than sitting here drinking expensive champagne by herself and ogling a handsome, dark-haired stranger—and a cowboy to boot.

Okay, this was *so* not like her. She was going to have to motion for the waiter, ask for her bill and then head back to the hotel.

Yet she couldn't seem to move. Instead she continued to wonder who the cowboy was and what brought him to El Jardin.

Maybe he was waiting for someone—a woman, most likely.

He lifted his longneck bottle and took a swig, then glanced toward the doorway as though he really was expecting someone to join him.

Jillian certainly hoped so. Because if he wasn't, if he was unattached, if he came over to her table…

She wasn't sure what she'd do.

Shane Hollister couldn't take his eyes off the classy blonde who sat all alone, practically begging for a guy to mosey on up and ask if she'd like some company.

She'd caught him looking at her on several occasions, too. And each time, he'd been tempted to toss her a smile. But he'd kept a straight face, since the last thing he needed today was for her to get the wrong idea and send a drink his way.

Or worse yet, invite him to join her.

Not that he wouldn't be sorely tempted. After all, she was attractive—the kind of woman some men—especially the insecure and weak type—might put on a pedestal.

Shane usually avoided women like her. Those classy

beauties were high maintenance and a lot more trouble than a common man wanted to deal with, especially today.

He glanced again at the entrance, a habit he'd acquired during his years as a detective with the Houston Police Department.

His waitress, a dark-haired woman in her early thirties, offered him a smile and nodded toward his nearly empty bottle. "Can I get you another beer?"

"Sure."

Again, his gaze was drawn to the blonde drinking champagne.

Maybe she was waiting for someone. Cristal, even a split, was a pricey order for someone to consume alone.

Of course, by the looks of that fancy handbag she carried and the clothes she was wearing, he had a feeling that price was the last thing she considered when making a purchase. Even her hair and makeup appeared to have been styled and applied by professionals.

In fact, everything about her implied grace and class, from a sizable pair of diamond earrings, to the trendy, rainbow-colored jacket she wore over a black top and slacks, all of which had to be designer wear.

But even with the bling or the extra effort she'd put into her wardrobe, hair and makeup, he had a feeling she'd look just as stunning in worn cotton and faded denim.

The cocktail waitress was more his type, though—more down-to-earth and approachable. That is, if he wanted to hook up with a woman instead of heading over to his brother's house for his nephew's birthday party late this afternoon.

If truth be told, though, he wasn't all that eager to face the squealing kids, with sticky hands and chocolate on their faces. Not that he didn't love them, but ever since he'd lost his son, it had torn him up to be around children.

And that was why he'd decided to have a beer before facing the Hollister clan today.

Of course, he didn't usually frequent fancy places like El Jardin, but he'd had some papers to sign at the escrow office down the street and decided to stop here, since it wasn't likely he'd be offered anything stronger than a soda when he arrived at Jack's house.

Ever since Joey's death, Shane's big, extended family—none of whom had been teetotalers—had cut way back on alcohol consumption, at least whenever Shane was around.

Okay, so he'd gone over the deep end for a while and they'd thought his drinking had become problematic. He doubted any of his siblings would have handled the grief any differently than he had back then. Besides, he'd taken control of his life again.

He glanced at his wristwatch. He probably ought to call back the cocktail waitress and cancel his order. Yet for some reason, he turned back to the sophisticated blonde who was spending a lot more time studying the elegant flute in her hand than drinking from it—when she wasn't looking his way.

There was something going on between the two of

them, and whatever it was held a bit of a promise, at least for the here and now.

If Shane hadn't already agreed, albeit reluctantly, that he'd make a showing at little Billy's birthday party, he might flash her a smile and come up with some clever way to strike up a conversation—something that didn't sound like a worn-out pickup line.

As it was, he'd better leave well enough alone. He was more cowboy than cop these days, and she didn't seem to be the kind of woman who would find either very appealing.

Still, he continued to glance across the room for what he swore would be the very last time.

She wore a lonely expression on that pretty, heart-shaped face. Her frown and the crease in her brow suggested she carried a few burdens herself.

Was she running from her own demons, too?

Or was she just thinking about another lonely Friday night?

Before he could even attempt his best guess, a guy seated near her table got to his feet, swaying a bit before starting toward her.

Shane's protective nature sparked, and he sat upright in his seat, listening as the guy spoke loud enough for the whole room to hear.

"Hey, come on, honey. Don't you want some company?"

The blonde stiffened and said something to the guy. Shane couldn't hear her words, but he suspected they'd been something short and to the point.

On the other hand, her body language spoke volumes, and only an idiot—or a drunk—would ignore it.

Sure enough, the snockered fool pulled out the chair next to hers and took a seat, clearly ignoring her verbal response, as well as all the outward signs of her disinterest.

Shane expected her to put the jerk in his place, but she looked to the right and left, as if searching for the waiter. What she needed was a bouncer, although Shane doubted a place like El Jardin had to use the services of one very often.

Did he dare try to come to her rescue?

Oh, what the hell.

He got to his feet, grabbed his hat—leaving his beer behind—and sauntered to the pretty blonde's table, determined not to make a scene.

"Hi, honey," he said. "I'm sorry I was late. Did you have to wait long?"

"I...uh..." She searched his eyes as if trying to figure out what he was doing, where he was going.

He reached out his hand to her, and she studied it for a moment, not understanding what he was trying to do—and that was to avoid causing a scene that was sure to draw unnecessary attention to her. But she seemed to catch on, because she took his hand and allowed him to draw her to her feet.

"I didn't think my meeting would take so long," he said.

"I understand. I knew you'd come as soon as you could get away."

Shane brushed a kiss on her cheek, then turned to the drunk. "Excuse me, but that's my seat."

"I…" The drunk furrowed his brow, then got to his feet. "Well, hell. She should've said something."

Shane narrowed his eyes. "She *did*. But maybe you didn't hear her."

"Yeah, well, maybe you shouldn't leave a woman like her waiting. It makes people think she's free for the taking."

Shane's right hand itched to make a fist, but the guy wasn't going to remember any of this tomorrow. And El Jardin wasn't the kind of place that lent itself to bar-room brawls.

"Speaking of free for the taking," Shane said, "I'm going to give you some good advice."

"What's that?"

"It's time to call it a day."

As the waiter who'd been working this side of the bar approached, he asked the blonde, "Is there a problem here?"

She looked at Shane, who nodded at the drunk. "This gentleman is going to need a cab."

Within seconds, the manager of the bar entered the picture, and the drunken businessman was escorted away.

"Thank you," the blonde told Shane. "I wasn't sure what to do about him without making a scene."

"No problem."

"They should have quit serving him a long time ago," she added.

"You're right. And your waiter is getting an earful from his boss as we speak."

"What makes you say that?"

"By the look the manager shot at him when he realized how drunk that guy was."

"I didn't notice that."

He shrugged. "I'm observant by nature."

"Well, I'm glad you stepped in when you did."

"Me, too."

Now what? he wondered.

Well, he'd gone this far, so why not?

He glanced at the empty chair across from her. "Is that seat taken?"

It was a lame line, he supposed, but it was the best he could come up with at the moment.

"No, it's not. Would you like to join me?"

Well, how about that? He'd made it to first base. Before pulling out the chair, he extended his hand in greeting. "My name is Shane Hollister."

"Jillian Wilkes." As their palms met and her fingers slipped around his, a warm thrill shimmied up his arm and sent his senses reeling.

He had to force himself to release her hand, and as he did so, they each took a seat.

As much as he hated pickup lines and all the small talk that went into meeting someone for the first time, he realized there wasn't any way around it.

"So what brings you to El Jardin?" he asked.

"I came for a glass of champagne." She smiled, as though that made perfect sense, but the detective who still lived somewhere deep within found that hard to believe.

She must have read the question in his gaze, because her demeanor grew shy and uneasy.

Why? he wondered, more curious about her than ever. What was her story? Why would a woman like her be in a sophisticated bar all by herself?

Shane glanced at the nearly full bottle. "Are you celebrating a birthday or something?"

"Actually, yes. My divorce is final today."

He nodded, as though that was a perfectly good reason to drink alone. Heck, he'd downed nearly a bottle of whiskey after his.

Jillian didn't appear to be tying one on, though. He hadn't seen her take more than an occasional sip. It must be some kind of mock celebration, which suggested the breakup hadn't been her idea.

If not, what kind of man let a woman like her slip through his fingers? Or was there more to Jillian Wilkes than just a pretty face and graceful style?

Was she a spendthrift? Or someone who didn't appreciate a man's family or his job?

Shane could relate to that, but he wasn't planning to talk about his past, let alone think about it. So he turned the conversation back to her. "How long were you married?"

"Nearly eight years."

"Kids?"

A shadow darkened those sea-blue eyes. "No."

Had they split for that reason? Some people wanted children; others didn't.

He regretted his curiosity, yet couldn't shake the raging interest. "Something tells me you're only putting on a happy face."

She twisted a silky strand of hair in a nervous fashion. "I'll be okay. *Really.* And to be honest, I'm looking forward to the changes my new life will bring."

"Was the divorce your idea?" Shane didn't know why it mattered. But it did.

"I had higher expectations from the marriage than he did." She shrugged, then said, "I believe that promises should be kept, that marriages are meant to last and that people in love need to honor and protect each other from heartbreak, not dish it out."

The guy must have screwed around on her. If so, he was a fool. Or so it seemed. "He left you for someone else?"

"A lot of somebodies." She lifted her glass, took a sip.

He watched the movements in her throat as she swallowed, amazed at how something so simple, so basic, could practically mesmerize him and send his blood humming through his veins.

She leaned forward. "And what about you, Shane?"

What about *him?*

He wasn't about to spill his guts. Still, her self-disclosure was a little refreshing, and he found himself admitting, "I *was* married, but not anymore."

"Do you mind if I ask why not?"

Yeah, he minded. He'd rather keep things focused on her and on why she was here. On the soft sound of her voice, the stunning blue of her eyes, the graceful way she sat before a glass of champagne and hardly took a drink.

But he supposed it wouldn't hurt to be honest.

"My ex-wife didn't like my job," he admitted.

She'd also resented his family. But he kept part of the equation to himself.

"What do you do for a living?" Jillian asked.

He hesitated before answering. "I'm a ranch hand on a little spread about two hours from here. But when I was married, I had a job that kept me away from home a lot."

He'd also had a competent—and beautiful—female partner who'd managed to gain the respect of the entire precinct, and a wife who'd been jealous of the time they'd spent together, even though it had always been work-related. But there really wasn't any reason to go into that.

"My husband," she began, "or rather, my *ex*-husband, traveled on business, too. But I hadn't bargained on his infidelity while he was on the road, and I refused to forgive him for it."

Something in her eyes, in the gentle tone of her voice, convinced him she was being honest.

Again, his conscience rose up, suggesting he unload his whole story on her. But what was the use? He knew nothing would amount from this…whatever *this* was. A mere conversation, he supposed. A pleasant diversion for two battered ships passing on a lonely night.

It was too early to predict anything more. And with him living and working two hours away in Brighton

Valley... Well, there wasn't much chance of *this* becoming anything else.

She leaned forward. "Can I ask you a question?"

"Sure, go ahead." But Shane couldn't guarantee an answer.

"Do all men cheat?" Those brilliant tropical-blue eyes nailed him to the back of his seat. "Did *you?*"

The raw emotion bursting from her question—both of them, actually—took him aback, but he was glad he could be open and honest with her, at least about that. "I suppose a lot of men are tempted, and some give in to it. But I didn't."

He'd been brought up in the church and had been an altar boy, which didn't necessarily mean anything. But more important, his parents had been happily married for nearly forty years. Divorce had never seemed like an option to him. And neither had lying to or cheating on a spouse.

"I'm glad to hear that." She slid him a pretty, relief-filled smile, as if he were some kind of hero.

A man could get used to having a woman look at him like that. And while Shane had never really thought of himself as particularly heroic, even when he'd been one of Houston's finest, it was nice to be appreciated for the values he did have.

"I don't suppose you'd like to join me for dinner," she said.

Her suggestion, which was more than a little tempting, knocked him off kilter, especially since he had other plans.

He didn't need to look at his watch again to know

that it was time for him to head across town to Jack's house for that party. Nor did it take much for him to envision a houseful of kids on sugar highs.

But that kind of scene didn't bother him too much. What really got to him, what shook him to the core, was the sight of an infant nursing at its mother's breast or a toddler bouncing on daddy's knee.

He loved his nieces and nephews—even the babies. He really *did*. It's just that whenever he was around them, he was reminded of his loss and his pain all over again.

"It would be my treat," Jillian said, those azure eyes luring him to forget what he'd set out to do in Houston today—and soundly winning the battle.

"Either I pay for dinner or we split it," he said. "I'm old-fashioned about things like that."

"All right. We'll split it, then." She blessed him with an appreciative smile. "I've never liked eating alone."

Riding solo—at meals or through life—had become a habit for Shane, but right now, he was looking forward to spending a little more time with Jillian, even if he knew that's as far as things would go.

"Where do you want to have dinner?" he asked.

"I have a room at a hotel down the street. Why don't we eat there?"

In her room?

Or at the hotel?

"They have a couple of nice restaurants to choose from," she added.

Okay, so she hadn't issued a dinner-with-benefits invitation.

"Eating at the hotel sounds good to me."

Besides, if the stars aligned just right, the hotel would certainly be…convenient.

And for some reason, Shane was feeling incredibly lucky tonight.

Chapter Two

Nearly four weeks later, Jillian stood in the small bathroom of her apartment and stared at the results of the home pregnancy test she'd purchased earlier that day.

Her tummy clenched as she watched a light blue plus sign grow darker and brighter, providing the news she couldn't quite grasp.

Pregnant?

How could that be? Surely there was a mistake.

She blinked twice, hoping that her vision would clear, that the blue would fade to white, that the obvious result in front of her wasn't real. But the truth was impossible to ignore. She conceived a baby the one and only time she'd slept with a stranger.

"This can't possibly be happening," she said aloud,

as if she could actually argue with reality. "We used protection that night."

But her words merely bounced off the pale green bathroom walls.

Was an unexpected pregnancy fate's way of punishing her for an indiscretion she'd never have again?

If so, it didn't seem fair. After all, it wasn't as if she'd set out to find someone to help her make it through the first night of her post-divorce life. She'd been too caught up in the legal and emotional aspects of the paperwork she'd just signed, the small settlement she'd received and the pain of Thomas's betrayal to even give a new relationship a second thought.

She blew out a ragged sigh, still unable to tear her eyes away from the test results that taunted her.

The irony of it all amazed her. Thanks to Shane's quiet departure from her room that night, they'd completely avoided the typical "Now what?" questions that usually cropped up after two consenting adults had sex for the first time. But here she was, facing an ever bigger "Now what?" on her own.

Having a baby was going to change her plans to get a teaching credential and land a job right afterward. How did she expect to support herself and a child while attending school? And day care for an infant was very expensive.

"A *baby?*" she whispered. As much as she'd always wanted to be a mother, she couldn't help thinking that the timing was off—way off.

She placed the palm of her hand on her flat stomach and tried to imagine the enormous changes facing her now.

Another woman might have considered all of her options, especially adoption, but Jillian felt she would just have to figure out a way to make it all work out.

Somehow, some way, she would come to grips with her pregnancy and motherhood. She'd have to.

She moved her hand upward, from her womb to her heart, where the beat quickened as reality began to sink in.

Should she call someone? She certainly could use a confidant right now.

In the past, whenever she'd had a crisis, she'd go to her grandmother for advice. Gram had always been there for her. When Jillian had learned that Thomas had been cheating, Gram had been the one she'd turned to, the one who'd offered her full support.

"I know this hurts now," Gram had said, "but you're going to come out on top of all this. You're a survivor. You'll meet someone else someday, someone who truly deserves you."

At the time, while the idea of meeting a white knight in shining armor had put a glimmer of hope back in her heart, Jillian had feared that her marriage to Thomas might have left her skeptical of even the most loyal and honest of men.

Maybe that's why she'd invited Shane back to her hotel room that night—in the hope that her white knight wore a Stetson.

Look where *that* move had gotten her.

Jillian still couldn't seem to wrap her mind around

the fact that her whole world was about to take a dramatic turn toward the complete unknown. Yet a tiny, comforting smile made its way to her lips. Finally, after years of hoping and praying that she'd conceive a child with Thomas, she was going to have a baby on her own.

Gram would be over the moon to learn that there was going to be a little one to cuddle and love, but she was also very old-fashioned. Hearing that Jillian had slept with her baby's father on their one and only date, especially when Jillian knew very little—well, practically nothing—about the man, wouldn't sit well with her. For that reason alone, Jillian didn't have the courage to call Gram and request advice on her latest "little problem."

The details of her baby's conception probably ought to bother Jillian, too, and while she felt a bit embarrassed by having a one-night stand, she wasn't going to beat herself up over what she'd done.

She'd realized at the time that she might eventually regret her decision to invite Shane back to her hotel room. Yet even the next morning, when she'd awakened in bed and found him gone, her only regret had been that she would never experience love in his arms again.

Even now, standing in the middle of her bathroom, awed by everything that little blue plus sign represented, she couldn't help thinking back on the morning after their night together, when she should have felt regret—and hadn't.

The scant light of dawn had just begun to peek through a gap in the curtains, when she'd stretched awake in the king-size bed, the memory of an incredible night slowly unfolding.

Shane's hands sliding along her curves, hers exploring his well-defined biceps, his muscular chest...

Bodies responding, arching, reaching a breath-stealing peak...a powerful climax, the likes of which she'd never known.

A slow smile had stolen across her lips as she'd reached for the naked cowboy lying beside her...only to feel the cool sheets across an empty mattress.

For a moment, in her sleep-fogged mind, she'd wondered if the amazing sex had just been a dream. But as she'd sat up in bed and opened her eyes, the covers had slipped to her waist, and the morning air had whispered across her bare breasts.

She'd blinked several times, then scanned the bedroom of her hotel room, looking for evidence of the handsome cowboy she'd met the night before. But she'd found no sign of him—no clothes, no hat, no boots.

As she'd surveyed the king-size bed on which she sat, the comforter that had slipped to the floor during the night and the rumpled sheets, she'd realized she hadn't been dreaming. Just to be sure, she'd reached for one of the pillows on the other side of the bed, lifted it to her nose and breathed in the masculine scent he'd left behind, the proof that he'd really been with her.

Yes, she'd realized. Shane Hollister had been the real deal, and the events that had sparked it all began to unfold in her mind. The slow dance they'd shared, the sweet words he'd whispered above the music, *Your ex-husband was a fool, Jillian.*

The arousing kiss that had followed…

The haze of heat and passion…

As the memory grew stronger, she recalled threading her fingers through his hair, pulling his lips closer, his tongue deeper. And when the kiss had gotten too hot to handle, she'd taken him by the hand and led him to her room.

No, their night together had been so much more than a dream.

And now?

She glanced down at the pregnancy test that announced she was facing yet another life-altering change.

Again, she thought about calling someone, a friend maybe. But she certainly couldn't reach out to any of the women who were still part of the Wilkeses' social circle.

Katie Harris, Jillian's college roommate, came to mind. Years ago, the two of them had been exceptionally close, but they'd drifted apart after graduation.

Jillian had meant to remedy that situation as soon as she was settled in her new place, although she hadn't gotten around to it yet. She could make that call now, of course, but she didn't want their very first chat to be an embarrassing tell-all. So when she did take the time to connect with Katie, she would keep her news and her dilemma to herself, at least for a while.

What about Shane? she wondered. Telling him was probably the right thing to do. But could she even find him?

Leaving the pregnancy test on the bathroom counter,

she went to her bedroom and opened the bureau drawer, where she'd put the note Shane had propped against the bathroom mirror before leaving her room that morning.

On the hotel letterhead, he'd written:

Dear Jillian,

I can't begin to thank you for a wonderful evening. I nearly woke you when I had to leave, but you looked so peaceful lying there that I didn't have the heart to disturb your sleep.

Last night was amazing. You were a gift I didn't deserve, and one I'll always cherish.

If you're ever in my neck of the woods, look me up. My friend and boss, Dan Walker, owns a spread that's located near Brighton Valley. He'll know how to contact me.

Either way, thanks for a memorable evening.
Shane

Jillian held the note for a while, studying the solid script, the bold strokes. She'd kept it as a souvenir of the magical night she'd spent with a cowboy. But now? It was all she had left of the man.

Well, that and the baby growing in her womb.

She could look him up, she supposed. And while tempted to do just that, she had to face the facts. What they'd shared had been far more therapeutic than a glass of champagne could ever be, but it was just a one-night thing. Anything else was wishful thinking on her part.

After all, she'd already given up her dreams for one man. There was no way she'd ever do that again.

Besides, what could possibly develop between her and a cowboy? Other than the physical intimacy they'd shared that night, they were pretty much strangers to each other.

Still, there was a baby to consider.

A wave of apprehension washed over her. Did she have to tell him? Would he even want to know?

She wasn't sure, but there wasn't any reason to make a game plan right this minute. Not when she was still struggling with the news herself.

A *baby*.

Once again, she placed her hand on her stomach, over the womb in which her little one grew. She had no idea what tomorrow would bring, but one thing was certain: She would raise her baby in a loving home, no matter what kind of man its daddy proved to be.

But there was something else she had to consider. Having a child together gave them far more in common than she'd even been able to imagine in the heat of the moment.

And whether she liked it or not, it was only fair to tell Shane he was going to be a father.

After a long day at the ranch and a stop at the cellular-phone store, Shane made the fifteen-minute drive home, dog-tired and muscles aching.

He'd no more than pulled his key from the front door when his new cell phone vibrated. So he pulled it out of his pocket and answered without checking the number on the display.

Out of habit, he answered, "This is Hollister."

"Shane, it's Jack."

His brother never called just to shoot the breeze. "Is something wrong?"

"I don't know. You tell *me*. We haven't heard from you in weeks. Hell, I've tried to cut you some slack after all you've been through, but things are getting worse. You've become really inconsiderate."

"Now, wait a second, little brother. I might not be living in Houston these days, playing golf with you guys and eating Sunday dinner, but I've been busy—not inconsiderate."

"Oh, no? Last month, you missed Billy's birthday party. You told us you'd stop by, but you never even showed up."

Shane turned on the lamp and shut the door, locking it for the night. "Something came up at the last minute, and I couldn't make it."

"Yeah, well you should have called to let someone know. We were worried about you."

"I *did* call, and Evan answered. I guess he didn't give you the message."

"Evan's only six years old, Shane. He can't be trusted to take messages."

"I figured that, so I asked him to put you or his mom on the line, but apparently he was too busy chasing after Emily to give the phone to someone older, so he told me to call back later." Shane took a seat on the chair nearest to the door and kicked off his dusty boots.

"Okay, so you're off the hook for the no-show at the birthday party," Jack said, "but I've tried calling you several times today, and your phone never even rang through."

"I lost my cell and wasn't able to replace it until about twenty minutes ago."

"Where'd you lose it?"

"If I knew that, then it wouldn't be lost, would it?"

Jack blew out an exasperated sigh. "All right. So that was a dumb question. But what was so important that you couldn't make it to Billy's party?"

Shane had never been one to kiss and tell. He supposed he could say that he'd met a woman and leave it at that, which would have pleased Jack and the rest of the family no end. But meeting a woman implied that he'd found her promising enough to keep seeing her, which wasn't exactly the case.

Yet Jack didn't need to know any of that. The only way to keep him in the dark was to stretch the truth, which wasn't the same as lying, but still went against Shane's grain. "Let's just say that I met an old friend, and the time just slipped away."

"A *female* friend."

Shane couldn't blame Jack for hoping that Shane had met someone special, but that hadn't happened.

"Who is she?" Jack asked, connecting the dots.

But Shane didn't want to go into it—any of it. Jillian had been more than a one-night stand. She'd been a one-night memory, and he wasn't about to share the details with anyone.

"It wasn't a woman," Shane lied. "I met up with an old friend, a guy I used to work with."

The first stretch of the truth had seemed necessary,

but the actual lie gnawed at his conscience. Shane had always been straight up with his family and the people he cared about. But there really hadn't been another way around it if he wanted to maintain his privacy and keep the details from becoming Facebook fodder for the Hollisters, who were into that sort of thing.

Shane set aside his boots, then crossed the living room to the kitchen area.

"Well, you still ought to call home once in a while and let us know you're still alive and kicking. Hell, you could be laying in a morgue as a John Doe for all we know."

This was *Jack* speaking? The same brother who'd gone off to college and hadn't called home until their parents had complained to the Dean of Students?

"You're going to have to start over," Shane said. "What's the real problem here?"

"Hell, Shane. I know you're busy. But Mom's been worried about you. She hasn't seen you in months or heard from you in weeks."

Shane, who'd just reached for a glass in the kitchen cupboard, paused for a beat—long enough to flinch from a jab of guilt. Then he released a wobbly sigh. "I didn't realize it had been so long, Jack. Tell her I'm fine and not to worry about me. Riding herd is a lot easier— and safer—than chasing the bad guys in Houston."

"Tell her yourself. She's been lighting candles and going to mass all week. Under the circumstances, what with knowing how much you liked being a cop, she's stressing about your mental health."

Shane tensed. Sylvia Dominguez, his former partner, had been a little worried about the same thing—at least for a while. And he couldn't really blame her or his family for being concerned. He'd gone a little crazy a while back, after he'd been put on suspended duty for letting his heart, his grief and his temper get away from him. But after a sobering confrontation with his dad, he realized what he was doing to himself. So he stopped closing down bars and started facing his demons instead.

Facing them?

Yeah, right. That's why his old life was in Houston and he was living in a cramped studio apartment more than two hours away. It was also why it took forever to fall asleep at night.

Of course, the insomnia might be a thing of the past now that he had thoughts of pretty Jillian to chase away the nocturnal shadows that kept the sandman at bay.

He wondered how long that was going to last.

A lot longer than their short time together, he hoped.

"Did you hear me?" Jack asked.

"Yeah." And he'd already forgotten what they'd been talking about. "I'm just a little scattered tonight. I've got a lot on my mind."

"You don't owe me an explanation, but Mom's another story."

"Tell her that my mental health is fine," Shane said. "It's amazing what a change of scenery will do."

"I'm glad to hear it. But don't be a stranger."

"I'm sorry. I'll try to check in more often."

Jack paused a beat, then added, "If you ever need anyone to talk to, you know I'm here for you."

This particular brother was a good listener, as well as a peacemaker. So in the Hollister family, that made him invaluable.

"You never should have let Cindy talk you out of the priesthood," Shane said. "You would have made a good one."

Jack laughed. "Maybe so. But give Mom a call, will you?"

Shane glanced at his wristwatch. "It's nearly nine o'clock on a Thursday night. She's probably down at the parish playing bingo."

"You don't need to call tonight. But after that mess with Internal Affairs and your leave of absence, she's been stressing something awful. You know how it is."

Yeah, he did. And he hadn't meant to cause her any more grief. He'd put the family through enough already, which had been another good reason to leave Houston.

Hoping to change the subject, he asked, "How's everyone else doing?"

"Good, for the most part. Colleen's on the dean's list at Baylor again. Stevie left for the police academy yesterday. And Mary-Lynn's expecting again."

"Is Dad doing all right?"

"Yeah, but he'd like to hear from you, too."

"I'll call home in the morning."

After disconnecting the line and putting the receiver back in the charger, Shane plunked a couple of ice cubes into his glass, filled it full of tap water and took a nice, long swig.

Any other night, he might have been tempted to fix himself a *real* drink, but memories of Jillian were still too fresh in his mind. And despite their time together being purposefully short, it was also the kind of memory that was worthy of keeping…sacred in a way. And Shane wasn't about to lessen or cheapen it.

Those magical hours spent in her bed had been a once-in-a-lifetime experience, one he'd been reluctant to end.

As dawn had threatened to break over Houston, he'd drawn her close to his chest and savored the fragrance of her shampoo, the faint floral whiff of her perfume.

She'd slept with her bottom nestled in his lap, and he'd felt himself stirring, rising to the occasion—again. But even if they hadn't gone through the only condom they'd had during the night, time hadn't been on his side.

As he'd glanced through an opening in the heavy curtains and seen the night fading into dawn, he'd carefully slid his arm from under her head, trying his best not to wake her. Because a cowboy didn't call in sick, especially if the only excuse he had was a beautiful woman in his bed. So he'd snatched his wrinkled shirt and jeans from the floor.

He'd found himself dragging his feet, not wanting to go, not ready to end what they'd shared.

Why had it felt as though they'd created some kind of invisible bond, some reason for him to linger?

Probably because their lovemaking had been so good. That had to be it.

Besides, Shane wasn't ready for a relationship. And he wasn't sure if he ever would be again.

So he'd quickly gotten dressed, wishing he could

think of a better way to say goodbye. But he hadn't been able to come up with anything that wouldn't have created some kind of promise he couldn't keep. And that wouldn't have been fair to her.

Not that he didn't *want* to see her again. But they had very little in common, and their lives were headed in different directions.

His only regret had been slipping out of her bed at nearly five in the morning and leaving a note, which might have cheapened the whole thing.

Last night was amazing, he'd written. *You were a gift I didn't deserve, and one I'll always cherish.*

And while he'd struggled to choose the right words, he'd meant every one of them.

He supposed he could try to find her again. His detective skills and his connections wouldn't make it too hard. But Jillian wasn't the kind of woman who'd fit into Shane's life, whether it was in Houston or Brighton Valley.

He'd already gone through one star-crossed relationship that he shouldn't have let get off the ground, and he'd lost his son because of it.

No, he'd just have to let well enough alone. After all, if something between them was meant to be, then he'd run into her again. No need for him to chase after something that was sure to crash and burn.

But that didn't mean he wasn't sorely tempted to look her up in Houston. He'd love to spend one more night together.

They might end the evening in a blaze of glory, but what a way to go....

Chapter Three

In spite of knowing their time together had been a one-shot deal, Shane hadn't been able to get Jillian out of his mind.

Several times he'd actually thought seriously about looking her up in Houston. She hadn't given him a lot to go on, but he still had a few contacts at the police department who'd be able to help him out. Yet when push came to shove, he'd decided to let well enough alone.

That is, until he was urged to attend his niece's first communion in Houston on Sunday morning. After he'd missed Billy's birthday party a while back and created such a stir within the family, he'd decided to make a showing this time, even though he'd rather be anywhere than in a church on Sunday morning, especially if it required a confession.

It's not that he had some huge sin hanging over his head, but he wasn't ready to make things right with God when he still blamed the Big Guy Upstairs for allowing Joey to die. But he supposed he'd deal with that tomorrow morning.

Right now, he was headed to the city a day early, determined to see Jillian while he was there. Through his connections, he'd gotten her address just minutes ago: 237 Bluebonnet Court, apartment 16.

It had been exactly six weeks and a day since they'd met that magical evening in Houston, but the memory was still as strong and vivid as if it had only been yesterday.

After they'd split the bill that evening, Shane had insisted on being the one to leave a generous tip for the wait staff. Then he'd walked with her to The Rio, the hotel lounge that provided music and high-priced drinks to some of Houston's more exclusive crowd.

Shane wasn't used to hanging out at places like that, and he knew he'd been underdressed, but he'd been with Jillian, who belonged to that world.

"The music sounds good," she'd said.

At that point, being with her would make anything sound good. But she'd been right. The band was great.

As they'd made their way toward an empty table near the dance floor, Shane had placed his hand on the small of her back, claiming her in front of all the rich, fancy folks who'd gathered for an after-dinner drink.

She'd leaned against him and slid her arm around his waist in a move that seemed so natural, so right, that he wanted to hang on tight and never let go.

Then the music, something soft and slow, began to play and he hadn't been able to do anything other than to pull her into his embrace and dance cheek to cheek. As they'd swayed to a love song, as he'd inhaled her tropical scent, she'd melded into him as though they'd been made to dance with each other for the rest of their lives.

Something powerful had surged between them, something hot, soul stirring and arousing.

He'd taken her hand and brushed his lips across her wrist. As she'd looked at him, her lips parting, she'd gripped his shoulder as though her knees would have buckled if she hadn't.

And that's when he'd kissed her. Right there in the middle of that crowded dance floor.

As their lips parted, his tongue had sought hers, and they were swept away to some carnal place, where the music stopped and the room grew silent. At least, he could have sworn it had happened that way.

For a moment, he'd forgotten where they were, *who* they were. All he'd been aware of was a raging desire that promised to bring about something he'd never experienced before.

Then the music really did stop, and he'd come to his senses, albeit reluctantly. As he broke the kiss, he'd continued to hold Jillian tight, and with his lips resting near her temple, he'd confessed, "I don't normally do things like this."

"Neither do I."

As they'd slowly stepped apart, she'd closed her eyes

and, after taking a deep breath, said, "I...uh...have a room upstairs."

Shane hadn't been sure he'd heard right or if he'd somehow come to the wrong conclusion, so he'd waited a beat, hoping she'd spell it out for him. Then she did just that by taking his hand and leading him out of The Rio and to the elevators.

As the memory rolled on, just as it did each time a specific clip from that night began to play in his mind, he tried his best to shake it off. But damn. What an amazing evening that had been.

If truth be told, he'd been more than a little sorry that it had ended before he'd gotten a chance to see if a long-distance relationship between two people with nothing in common but great sex could actually work.

Now, as he gripped the steering wheel of his pickup and watched the street signs for Bluebonnet Court, the heated memory still remained front and center in his mind.

Of course, seeing her again didn't mean he was interested in starting a relationship. It was just a matter of satisfying his curiosity.

Would Jillian be glad to see him? Had she, too, found it impossible to forget all they'd shared that night?

Shane certainly hoped so. He'd just have to take things one step at a time.

As he turned and drove down the tree-lined street and approached a modest apartment complex, he wondered if the address he'd found for her was wrong. Jillian had been dressed to the nines and sporting diamonds when they'd met, and this neighborhood didn't seem like the part of town that would suit her taste or her designer pocketbook.

But there was only one way to find out.

He parked his truck in one of the spaces available for guests, then made his way to Jillian's apartment, hoping she was home.

And that she'd be glad to see him.

When the doorbell sounded, Jillian had been sitting on the sofa, reading over her college schedule. She hadn't been expecting company, and since she hadn't found time to meet any of the neighbors, she wasn't sure who it could be.

She had a feeling it might be her grandmother, though. Ever since Jillian had moved into the apartment, Gram had been stopping by with one surprise or another, such as kitchen gadgets, household necessities and decorator items.

Yesterday, she'd brought a framed watercolor print that she'd picked up at a garage sale, which was now hanging on the living room wall. That particular piece of art was a far cry from the expensive paintings and sculptures that had adorned the various homes Jillian had once shared with Thomas, but it reflected her new, simple lifestyle.

During the course of her marriage, Jillian had tried so hard to do everything Thomas and his family had expected her to do that she'd almost forgotten who she really was. So she was determined to reclaim herself and become the woman she should have been before Thomas Wilkes had come along. And creating a home for herself, decorated to her own taste and comfort, was part of the process.

Expecting to see Gram with another surprise in her arms, Jillian swung open the door with a smile. But when she spotted Shane Hollister, the smile faded and surprise took its place.

The cowboy was just as handsome as she remembered, maybe more so. And his smile, which was both boyish and shy, sent her senses reeling.

"I would have called first, but I didn't have your number." He lifted the brim of his hat with an index finger.

He hadn't had her address, either, but she was so stunned to see him again, so mesmerized by his familiar, musky scent, that she couldn't seem to find the words to respond or to question him.

But her gaze was hard at work, checking him out and soaking him in. He'd shaved, which had softened his rugged edge a bit, but he still wore a Stetson, jeans and boots—clearly a cowboy through and through.

"If this isn't a good time," he said, those luscious brown eyes glimmering as he broke the silence, "I can come back another day."

"No, it's not that." She stepped aside to let him in. "It's just that I…"

"…didn't expect to see me again?" He tossed her a crooked grin that darn near turned her inside out.

She managed a smile of her own. "How'd you find me? I didn't even have an address to give you when we met."

"It's amazing what a person can learn over the internet."

Jillian wasn't sure if she should be happy he'd found her or concerned by it. After all, she didn't know very much about him, other than the fact that he hadn't always been a cowboy, and that he was divorced.

And that he'd claimed to be a tumbleweed, while they'd had dinner that night, which was a little worrisome. If he was indeed prone to wander and not set down roots, he wouldn't be the kind of father she wanted for her baby. That alone had seemed like the perfect excuse not to contact him so far.

Not that she'd made a solid decision yet. She would need to know more about him before she could allow him to be involved in the baby's upbringing.

And as luck would have it, here was her chance. So she swept her arm toward the brown tweed sofa that had once been in Gram's den and the faux leather recliner that had belonged to her grandfather. "Have a seat."

"Thanks." He placed his hat on one side of the sofa, then sat on the middle cushion. "I hope I'm not interrupting anything."

Just her conscience and her good sense.

"No, not really." She combed her fingers through her hair, suddenly wondering what she looked like without any makeup, without having used a brush since this morning.

"I have a family function in Houston," he said, "so, while I was in the area, I thought I'd stop by and say hello. I also thought it might be nice to have dinner together."

The last time they'd shared a meal, she'd invited him to spend the night. Was he expecting the same thing to happen again?

She could certainly see where he might. When they'd danced in each other's arms at The Rio, the sexual attraction had ignited. She'd never had a one-night stand before, so she'd struggled with her conscience before inviting him up to her room. But only momentarily.

Once she'd had that sweet experience, she hadn't been sorry about it, either. Shane had been an incredible lover who'd done amazing things with his hands and his mouth, taking her places she'd never gone before. Ever.

If truth be told, she was sorely tempted to have him take her there again.

But look where sexual attraction and throwing caution to the wind had gotten her—pregnant with the cowboy's baby.

"What do you say?" he asked, clearly picking up on how torn she was between a yes or a no.

Getting involved with him again would certainly complicate her life, so she was tempted to decline and send him on his way. But what did she know about the man who'd fathered her baby? And what was she supposed to tell her child when he or she inevitably asked the daddy questions?

"We really don't have much in common," she admitted. Nothing other than a baby, of course.

"Well, we don't know that for sure. We never really had a chance to talk much that night."

He was right about that. Even though they'd known each other's bodies intimately, the rugged cowboy was pretty much a stranger to her—as she was to him.

But he'd also put her healing process on the fast track and had made her feel desirable again.

So did that make them friendly strangers?

Or strangers with benefits…?

Jillian fiddled momentarily with the silver pendant that dangled from her necklace, then made the decision. "All right. Let me freshen up and change my clothes."

His smile nearly took her breath away, as he leaned back in his seat. "No problem. Take your time."

Thirty minutes later, she and Shane entered a little Italian restaurant he'd recommended. She'd chosen to dress casually in black jeans and a pale blue sweater.

At least on the outside, she and Shane appeared to be a better match than they had before, but for some reason she felt like a late-blooming high school senior about to enter the adult world for the first time.

"This place isn't as nice as the hotel restaurant," Shane said, "but the food is out of this world."

Jillian took a hearty whiff of tomatoes and basil, not doubting Shane about the taste. "It sure smells good."

After the hostess seated them at a quiet table for two, a busboy brought them water with lemon and a basket of freshly baked bread.

"So what do you do for a living?" Shane asked.

Jillian had planned to be the first one to start asking questions, but she supposed they both had a lot to learn about each other. "Right now, I'm planning to go back to school, but I'll be looking for part-time work soon."

"What kind of job did you have before?"

She hated to admit that she'd never worked, even though she'd kept pretty busy. But she doubted that he'd care about her philanthropic endeavors—the hospital board on which she'd served or the women's club, of which she'd been the chair. She was proud of her contributions, of course, but her heart hadn't been in the projects that had been hand chosen by Thomas—or rather, by his mother. The trouble was, until recently, her volunteerism had been her life, her work. Her only legitimate purpose in the world.

For some reason, she felt as though she ought to apologize or make excuses while explaining that she had high hopes for the future. "I didn't have a regular job, but I did volunteer work for several charitable organizations over the past few years."

He seemed to mull that over for a moment, then reached for the bread basket, pulled back the linen cloth that kept it warm and offered her the first slice, which she took.

"So you're going to take some college classes?" he asked.

"I'm getting a teaching credential."

"Oh, yeah? You must like kids."

"I do."

"But, if I remember correctly, you don't have any of your own."

It wasn't actually a question, just a conclusion he'd

obviously come to after something she must have told him. She supposed there was no real reason to respond.

If truth be told, she'd always longed to have a baby—at least two or three. But she and Thomas had never been able to conceive—at least, not together.

And now here she was—unwed and pregnant.

The waiter stopped by to take their orders, which was a relief since she really didn't want to talk about babies with Shane right now. But her luck didn't hold.

Once they were alone again, he picked up right where he'd left off. "I guess teaching would be the next best thing to having kids of your own."

Not really. That thought hadn't even crossed her mind. Leaving kids out of the equation, she said, "Actually I'd like to be a high school English teacher."

Shane arched an eyebrow, his skepticism drawing another smile from her, even though she ought to be miffed that he seemed to be as cynical as Thomas had been when she'd first told him her plan to return to college and get her credential.

"Teenagers can be a real pain to deal with," he said. "Why not teach kindergarten or one of the lower grades?"

"Because I love the written word. And I'd like to make literature and grammar interesting to teenagers, especially those without college aspirations. I want to encourage them to reach their full potential." She studied his expression, hoping that he was merely questioning the age of the students she wanted to teach and not the work she wanted to do.

When he didn't seem to find her dream unusual or

unfitting, she added, "And not just any kids. I want
to work with bright but unmotivated teens from lower
socio-economic backgrounds who believe that college
is out of their reach."

"No kidding?"

She shrugged, waiting for him to give her the same,
patronizing response Thomas had when she'd shared
her plans with him.

Instead, he grinned, creating a pair of sexy dimples
in his cheeks. "I hated English in school, but with a
teacher like you, I would have tried a lot harder."

When he looked at her like that, when he smiled,
her heart soared in the same way it had the night they'd
met. Just being with him again and feeling the growing buzz of sexual awareness was enough to remind
her why she'd taken him back to her room, why she'd
given in to sweet temptation.

It didn't take a psychic to see that she'd be tempted
to take him to bed again, once he took her home.

So now what?

Why had he come looking for her? Was he interested
in making love one more time?

Or was he missing her, missing *this*—their time together?

Did he want to actually date her? And if so, how did
she feel about that?

Long-distance relationships didn't usually work out.
Not that Jillian was ready for anything like that to develop between them. After all, she'd made one mistake
by believing a man to be honorable when he wasn't. She

certainly didn't want to make another one by acting too soon.

Still, spending time with Shane was making her realize that she hadn't been permanently damaged by her husband's infidelity and that the right man *would* come along someday.

Would that man be Shane Hollister?

It was impossible to know after only two evenings together. Besides, she had the baby to consider. So she might as well feel him out about that.

"How about you?" she asked. "Do you have any children?"

The spark in his eyes dimmed, and he seemed to tense. For several long, drawn-out heartbeats, he held his tongue, and she felt compelled to apologize, to sympathize—to do or say something, although she didn't have a clue what.

Finally, he answered, "No, I don't."

Something in his tone, in his demeanor, made her wonder if he liked it that way. If so, how would he react when she finally told him about the baby? Would he be happy? Uneasy? Angry?

Would he worry about being responsible—financially or otherwise—for a child he'd never intended to have?

As curious as she was, as much as his answers mattered, she didn't push for more. She wasn't ready for a full-on discussion about babies or kids right now, so she opted to change the subject.

"You mentioned that you used to work in Houston. What did you do?"

He reached for his goblet of water, then took a drink.

Finally he said, "I worked for the Houston Police Department, first as a patrolman, then as a detective."

She wasn't sure what she'd expected him to say—that he'd been in sales, she supposed. Or that he'd had a dead-end job of some kind. But a police officer?

Not only did that surprise her, it made her feel a whole lot better about him and the man he was.

"Why did you quit?" she asked.

He grew quiet again, as if she'd unearthed something he didn't want to talk about. Then he shrugged. "It's complicated."

Which meant what? That she wasn't going to get any more out of him than that?

Who *was* Shane Hollister?

Before she could quiz him further, the waiter brought their food, lasagna for him and pasta primavera for her, creating a momentary lull in the conversation.

While Shane picked up his fork, Jillian asked again, this time point blank, "Why did you leave the police force?"

Shane dug into his lasagna and took a bite, hoping Jillian would get the hint that he didn't want to talk in detail about the past. There were too many mitigating factors that had caused him to leave the force, too much other stuff to reveal. And no matter how much he enjoyed her company, he wasn't ready to spill his guts yet. And he wasn't sure he'd ever be.

"Like I told you," he said, "it's complicated."

She waited a beat, yet didn't let up on him. "Okay, then tell me about yourself. Where were you born? What kind of childhood did you have?"

He supposed he couldn't blame her for being curious. He had a lot of questions for her, too.

"There's not much to tell," he said. "I was born in Houston and grew up as the youngest of three boys and two girls in a big, close-knit family."

She leaned forward, as if he'd told her something interesting. "It's nice that you have a big family."

He'd always thought so. He watched her spear a piece of broccoli with her fork. The candlelight glistened on the platinum strands of her hair, making her appear radiant and almost…angelic.

Unaware of his gaze, she looked up and smiled. "I never knew my father, so it was only my mom and me at first. After my mother died, I moved in with my grandparents. I'm afraid it's just Gram and me now."

Marcia had been an only child, too, which had made it nearly impossible for her to relate to a big, rambunctious family like the Hollisters.

Shane had a feeling Jillian would feel the same way if she ever met them. And that was just one more reason a relationship with her wouldn't work out.

But tell that to his hormones. Damn, she was a beautiful woman, even if she was mortal and prone to imperfections.

So why couldn't he spot any of them?

As she lifted her water goblet, brought it to her lips and swallowed, he followed the simple movement as it moved down her throat.

When he'd kissed her there that night, running his tongue along her neck and throat, she'd come alive in his arms.

Had the memory ingrained itself in her mind, too?

He kept reminding himself that they really weren't suited, but that didn't seem to matter right now.

"So what was it like growing up as one of five kids?" she asked, as if she had no idea he'd been ogling her from across the table.

"It was okay, I guess." He'd idolized his older siblings until his teenage years, when he'd found them bossy and a real pain in the ass. But in retrospect, he realized they'd just been looking out for him, even if they'd sometimes overstepped their boundaries.

He'd actually thought his family had been the typical, all-American variety until he married Marcia. She'd been annoyed by them and couldn't understand the closeness they'd shared. In fact, she'd thought they were intrusive and out of line most of the time.

It had made life pretty miserable for everyone, not just her and Shane.

But it had been more than his family that had bothered her. She'd hated his job, too.

When Shane was promoted to detective, his marriage seemed to get better because he'd received a pay increase and was no longer patrolling the city streets. He'd also known better than to vent about the ugliness that he saw nearly every day. Instead, he'd stretched the truth and made his job sound safe and routine.

But Marcia hadn't bought it. When she'd accused him of cheating on her with his partner—something he *hadn't* done—he'd finally thrown in the towel.

Shane wondered what Jillian would say if she knew how many of his family members worked in one law

enforcement field or another. Or if he told her that he'd
wanted to be a cop ever since he could remember and
that he'd once believed he'd been born to wear a badge.

Stuff like that hadn't mattered to Marcia. She'd
hated everything about his line of work, which was
why she'd eventually been the one to cheat, something
he'd learned after the fact.

"You're not very forthcoming," Jillian said.

He hadn't meant to clam up completely. "I'm sorry.
It's just that my ex-wife didn't like my family or my job.
So when you start asking me about either one of them,
I get a little defensive and cryptic. It's an old habit, I
guess."

"I'm sorry to hear that."

To hear what? That he had old baggage and habits?

He didn't want her to think that he was still dealing
with the aftereffects of his divorce. "For what it's worth,
I did everything I could think of to make my marriage
work. I went so far as to buy a house in a small town
about an hour or so from Houston, even though that
meant I'd have a big commute each day."

"It didn't help?"

"No, it was more than my family dynamics creating
problems. My ex used to push me to change careers, to
find a job that paid more money, a position that would
allow me to spend more time at home. But that was one
compromise I wasn't willing to make."

"So now you're a tumbleweed. You can come and
go as you please."

"Yeah, I guess you can say that."

She grew silent, and while he was tempted to get

the conversation back on track, he wasn't sure what to say that wouldn't lead him back to the things he didn't want to discuss. Like the losses he'd suffered—his wife through divorce, his son through death and his career by choice.

"I have a question I've been meaning to ask you," he said.

"What's that?" She picked up her napkin and blotted her lips.

He couldn't see any reason to tiptoe around it, so he came right out and laid it on the table. "Do you ever think about the night we met?"

Her gaze lifted from her plate, and as it locked on his, his heartbeat rumbled in his chest. In the silence, a thousand words passed between them.

"Sometimes," she admitted.

Her expression was far more revealing, and he suspected that her musings were more in tune to his own—and that she thought about what they'd shared in Houston more than she wanted him to know.

"So what do you want to do about it?" he asked.

She paused as though giving it some real thought, then bit down on her bottom lip before saying, "I don't know, Shane."

He could have pressed her at that moment, but to be honest, he wasn't sure if it would be in his best interest if he did. After all, they had very little in common and lived nearly two hours apart.

Instead, he picked up his fork and tried to convince himself that he had an appetite for pasta, cheese and marinara sauce, when he hungered for a lot more than food.

When they finished their meal, Shane paid the bill and they walked back to his pickup, the soles of their shoes crunching along the blacktop-covered parking lot.

So now what? he wondered. Where did they go from here?

He didn't ask, though. Not when he still questioned the wisdom of getting involved in a relationship that had a snowball's chance in hell. So he decided to bide his time and see how things played out.

Ten minutes later, they were standing at her door, with a lovers' moon overhead.

"I'm sorry for prodding you earlier," she said. "I didn't mean to pry or make you relive painful memories."

"I can't blame you for being curious. You don't know me very well."

"I know you better than I did before." She smiled up at him, revealing a shy side of herself, then reached into her purse for the keys. "I'm glad you looked me up."

Was she? Even though he hadn't been as "forthcoming" as she would have liked?

Truth was, neither of them had shared very much about themselves. Was that for the best?

Or was it an excuse to get together again?

"I'm glad I found you, too," he said.

"Thanks again for dinner."

So that was it? She was just going to let herself into the apartment and close the door?

He tried to tell himself that it was for the best, but he couldn't quite buy that with an amazing array of stars blinking overhead, with his blood pumping to beat the band, with her scent taunting him....

Unable to help himself, he skimmed his knuckles along her cheek, felt the warmth of her flush, heard the catch of her breath.

As her lips parted, his control faded into the phero-mone-charged air, and he lowered his mouth to hers.

Chapter Four

Just a whiff of Shane's manly cologne, with its hint of leather and musk, stirred up an exhilarating sense of adventure. And as their lips met, Jillian's heart soared with anticipation.

She'd convinced herself to take things slow and easy until she knew him better, but at the moment, she couldn't care less about that. Not when everything they'd shared before was about to happen all over again—the passion, the heat, the pleasure.

Oh, how that man could kiss!

He slipped his arms around her, and she leaned into him as if they'd never been apart. Their bodies melded together, and the kiss deepened until desire exploded into a blast of colors, reminding her why she'd thrown caution to the wind that incredible evening in Houston.

And something told her she wasn't going to be any stronger at fighting temptation now than she'd been back then.

She'd wanted to spend more time with him so she could learn just what kind of man he really was. But at this rate, she was only going to find out what kind of lover he was. And she already knew that Shane Hollister was the best ever.

As their tongues mated, as breaths mingled and mouths grew desperate, he pulled her hips against his growing arousal, and she pressed into him as if it was the most natural thing in the world to do.

Right there, on her porch, where all her neighbors could see, she kissed him as though there would be no consequences or tomorrows.

But there would be plenty of both if she let her hormones run away with her. Making love to him this evening would only complicate things further—if that was even possible. And she couldn't afford to do that again. Not until she had a chance to actually date the man.

So she placed her hands on his chest and slowly pushed back, ending the kiss.

"You have no idea how tempted I am to ask you inside," she said, her breath a bit raspy from the arousing assault on her senses. "But I'm on the rebound, and you might be, too. So for that reason—and a few others—I think it would be best if we took things a little slower."

"Maybe," he said, although something in his eyes suggested he wasn't convinced.

Yet in spite of his apparent acceptance of her words,

neither of them made a move to end their evening together.

She closed her eyes, caught up in a heady cloud of swirling pheromones, musky cologne and the vibrant and steady beat of a heart on the mend. As tempted as she was to ask him to stay the night, she had to let him go. She'd thrown caution and morals to the wind once, but she couldn't make a habit of it.

Not until she knew him better.

When she glanced up at him, he tossed her a crooked grin. Yet the hint of a shadow darkened his eyes, an emotion too fleeting for her to get a handle on.

She rested a hand on his chest, where his heart beat strong and steady. Surely she was being too cautious. But she couldn't quite bring herself to change the stance she'd taken.

"Do you have a piece of paper and pen?" he asked.

She reached into her purse and pulled out the small notepad she carried, along with the attached ink pen.

When she handed it to him, he scratched out his phone number on the top sheet, than gave it back to her. Deciding to provide him with hers, as well, she tore out a page from the back of the booklet, jotted down her number for him.

"Well…have a good evening," she said, although she suspected that they'd both have a better one if they didn't spend it alone.

Shane brushed another kiss on her lips, this one light and fleeting. He hesitated momentarily, as if he was struggling with something. Then he kissed her a third and last time, a heart-thumping, hope-stirring kiss that would linger in her memory long after he left.

As he walked to his truck, she stood at the door and watched him go.

She ached to call him back, but if she got in too deep and too soon, she would complicate not only her life, but her baby's. And she couldn't afford to do that yet.

There was, however, one thing that she did know. Meeting Shane and experiencing the thrill of a romance had completely dulled the pain of Thomas's betrayal. And she was tempted beyond measure to hang on to what they'd found together. But she couldn't enter a full-on affair with him. At least, not at this point.

As Shane climbed into his pickup, a feeling of remorse settled over her. It took all she had not to call him back—or run after him. But it was best this way, especially since she wasn't ready to tell him about the baby.

Still, as she went into the house and locked the door behind her, she couldn't help grieving what they might have shared tonight.

Shane spent the night on his parents' sofa, thanks to all the out-of-town family members who'd converged upon the house for Becky's first communion. He'd been surrounded by his nieces and nephews, who had spread their sleeping bags all over the floor.

The kids had gotten up at the crack of dawn, so he'd merely put his pillow over his head to block out the noise and the morning light.

He had no idea what time it was now—or where

they'd gone—but thankfully they were all up and at 'em.

Years ago, he'd thought that the old sofa was pretty comfortable, but he'd awakened with a crick in his neck this morning, which left him ready to snap at anyone or anything that crossed his path.

Okay, so it was more than a few aches and pains that had him out of sorts. He was flat-out disappointed that he hadn't been invited to stay with Jillian last night, although he had no one to blame but himself.

She'd struggled with the decision to send him on his way. He'd seen it in her eyes, heard it in her passion-laced voice.

If there'd ever been a couple who'd been sexually compatible, it was the two of them. So it wouldn't have taken much effort on his part to convince her to change her mind.

But the truth of the matter was that she was coming off a recent divorce, which meant that she was vulnerable—maybe even more than most women might be. She hadn't had to come out and say that, either. He'd seen that in her eyes, as well.

Only a jerk would have taken advantage of her, which was what he'd told himself last night while his conscience had warred with his libido.

"I'm on the rebound," she'd said. "And you might be, too."

That hadn't been entirely true. Shane had gotten over his divorce a long time ago.

Still, he'd been tempted to suggest that they put another temporary balm on two grieving hearts, although he'd decided against it. Why jump into anything when the future was so questionable?

Besides, if she ever came out to Brighton Valley, which was becoming home to him, she'd probably go into culture shock.

Of course, he'd been more than a little surprised to find her living in a modest apartment, instead of something ritzy. Especially since her jewelry and designer clothes suggested that she belonged in a much nicer place—and in a better part of town.

So what was with that?

He supposed it made sense that she would move closer to the university she planned to attend, but wouldn't she be happier in an upscale neighborhood?

Or had she entered El Jardin that day primed and looking for a man who had money?

Shane didn't like that particular train of thought. Had he been wrong about her?

Before he could give it any real consideration, Jack's six-year-old son ran up to him. "Hey, Uncle Shane. Can I come out to your ranch someday and ride a horse? My dad said he'd take me out there, if it's okay with you."

Shane didn't mind having Jack and his family come to Brighton Valley. It might even be fun to show them around and make a day of it. "It's not my ranch, Evan. But I can arrange a visit and a horseback ride."

"Cool! I'll tell my dad you said it was all right. Woo-hoo!"

With that, the boy dashed off, whooping it up.

Shane liked kids; he really did. But sometimes it was tough being around his nieces and nephews, especially when he couldn't help thinking that Joey would be four now and running around with them.

Using his fingers, he kneaded the stiff and sore muscles in his neck.

Once he'd attended that first communion and given his niece the charm bracelet he'd bought, he'd be history—and headed back to Brighton Valley.

In the meantime, after folding up the blanket he'd used last night, he went into the kitchen for a cup of coffee. There, he found his mom alone, standing over the stove and flipping hotcakes.

"Why are you doing all the work?" he asked as he walked up behind her and placed a kiss on her cheek.

She turned to him and smiled. "Because I enjoy having you kids home. And besides, it's Sunday morning, remember?"

"How could I forget?" His mom's special buttermilk pancakes had become a church-day tradition at the Hollister house.

"Pour yourself a cup of coffee," she said, "then get some hotcakes while they're fresh and warm."

She didn't have to ask him twice. After filling a mug and piling the pancakes on a plate, Shane took a seat at the table, where he added a slab of butter and maple syrup on top of his stack.

"Where is everyone?" he asked.

"John and Karen took Becky to the church. She's meeting up with a couple of her girlfriends there. Tom and your dad are outside, watching Trevor ride his bike. When you finish eating, you ought to join them."

Shane didn't respond either way. But for the past

two-and-a-half years he'd been treading along the perimeter of most family gatherings, on the outside looking in. And truthfully it was easier that way.

He glanced at his wristwatch. Church would be starting soon, which was great. He was eager to get this day over with so he could head back to the ranch where he belonged. At least, that's how he'd been feeling lately.

It was weird, too. Back at the ranch where he worked, Dan and Eva Walker had two sets of twins. And while Shane tried to avoid his nieces and nephews, he didn't feel the same way about the Walker kids, although he wasn't sure why.

Maybe because Marcia had always blamed the Hollisters for the trouble in their marriage. And maybe in a way, he'd blamed them, too. Ever since dealing with his wife's complaints, Shane had stepped out of the family fold. And that was long before Joey had died.

Damn. Maybe Jillian was right. Maybe he *was* still dragging around some old baggage from his divorce.

He lifted the mug of coffee, savored the aroma of the fresh morning brew, then took a sip.

Making love with Jillian—and having dinner with her again last night—had been refreshing and…healing.

When he was with her, things felt different—better. And he wasn't just talking about a simple case of attraction. He'd actually been able to shed the shadows that plagued him for hours on end.

But the only way he could imagine hooking up with Jillian was if he moved back to Houston and took up his old life.

However, Jillian didn't seem to be the kind of woman

who'd be interested in dating a cop—even if he wanted to go back to work for the HPD. And at this point, he really didn't.

There was something appealing about Brighton Valley and small-town life. He actually enjoyed riding fence and herding cattle.

Of course, Jillian didn't seem like the kind who'd be happy with a cowboy, either. A life in Brighton Valley would be foreign to a woman like her.

So why set himself up for failure? He'd already gone through one divorce because his wife hadn't been happy with the life he'd wanted to lead.

So why even ponder the possibility of a relationship with Jillian, either long distance or right next door?

Because, for one thing, he couldn't get her off his mind.

And because he doubted that he'd ever be more sexually compatible with another woman again.

What a shame that would be.

As he cut into his pancakes, which were growing cold, he wondered if it might be best to leave the possibility of a relationship with Jillian to fate. After all, she had his phone number, and he'd included the name of the ranch on which he worked in the note he'd left her at the hotel.

So she could find him if she really wanted to.

"I'm going to get ready for church," his mother said. "Can I get you anything else? Some OJ? More coffee?"

"No, I'm fine." Shane looked up from his plate and smiled. "Thanks, Mom."

"You're more than welcome, sweetie." She stood in

the center of the room for a moment, not moving one way or the other, then added, "It's nice to have you home."

He nodded, unable to respond out loud. How could he when he was counting the minutes before he could head back to Brighton Valley and to a different way of life?

"I know that you haven't felt comfortable here for a long time," she said.

Coming from her, the truth stung. And while he wanted to soften things, to imply that she was wrong or to blame it all on his ex-wife, he couldn't bring himself to lie. "It's complicated, Mom. But I'm working on it."

Her eyes misted, yet she managed a smile. "I can't ask for more than that."

Then she left him alone in the kitchen, wondering if he'd ever feel like a part of the Hollister clan—or even another family—ever again.

Or if he'd even want to.

Jillian hadn't seen or heard from Shane in several months—long enough for her to start college classes, visit an obstetrician and to finally share her pregnancy news with Gram.

She'd been right, of course. Gram had been thrilled to learn that Jillian was expecting, but she hadn't liked the idea of her raising a child on her own.

"What about the father?" Gram had asked. "Does he plan to be a part of the baby's life?"

"I'm not sure how he'll feel about that." Jillian had

no way of knowing what Shane's reaction would be. "He doesn't know yet."

"You haven't told him that you're pregnant?" The tone of Gram's voice had indicated both surprise and disapproval.

"Not yet," Jillian had admitted.

Gram had clucked her tongue. "A man deserves to know that he's going to be a daddy, Jilly. You can't keep something like that from him. It's not fair."

"I'm going to tell him. I'm waiting for the right time."

"When is that?" Gram had asked. "On your way to the delivery room?"

Jillian wouldn't wait that long, but Gram was right. She was running out of time.

Ever since the night Shane had come by her apartment in Houston, she'd been kicking herself for letting him go without making arrangements to see him again. After all, she could have suggested that he stop by the next day on his way back to Brighton Valley…but she'd just assumed that he would.

In fact, she'd waited close to the house all day, hoping he might show up or call, but he hadn't done either.

But maybe that was her fault, not his. She hadn't meant to give him the impression that she wasn't interested in him. She'd just wanted to take things slow, to give herself some time to think.

Had he gotten the idea that she was shutting him out completely?

Or had he backed off, only to find another woman who interested him? Someone local and more his type?

That possibility sent a shiver of uneasiness through her. Had she found a knight in shining armor, only to let him slip through her fingers?

Sleeping with the handsome cowboy had just... happened. Well, that wasn't exactly true. That evening had unfolded as beautifully as a well-choreographed waltz.

She'd never been so spontaneous before, never been so bold as to suggest sex with a virtual stranger. But neither had she ever wanted to make love so badly with a man that nothing else had mattered.

If she'd actually gone to the hospital complaining of a broken heart or shattered dreams, Shane Hollister would have been just what the doctor would have ordered. He'd been sweet, sensitive, funny...and refreshing.

His kisses had been a better fix than any drug could have been; they'd made her feel whole and lovable again.

For the first time since learning of her ex-husband's infidelity, Jillian had found a way to ease the pain and to chase away the emptiness she'd lived with for months—if not for all the years she'd been married. And in the midst of it all, Shane had taken her to a place she'd never been before, a peak and a climax she'd never even imagined.

How could she not want to see him again?

More than once, she'd been tempted to call him. Yet she hadn't, which meant that Shane Hollister continued to be a mystery. Each time she'd picked up the phone, she'd chickened out.

The longer she waited, the harder it was going to be. So she would contact him today.

Didn't she owe him that much?

She reached for her purse and searched for the small notepad on which he'd written his number. It had been several months since he'd given it to her.

What if he'd gotten involved with someone else in the meantime?

Her heart cramped at the thought, creating an ache she hadn't been prepared for. After all, it's not as though she had any claim on him.

Oh, no?

She placed her hand on the swell of her belly, where their baby grew, and her thoughts drifted back to the night she'd taken him to her hotel room.

She'd never done anything so bold or brazen before and doubted that she ever would again. But *she* hadn't been sorry then, and she wasn't sorry now.

In less than five months she would be having Shane's baby. She was going to have to tell him, no matter what the consequences were. And it was only right to do that in person.

So she pulled out the notepad where he'd written his number. The page curled up on the ends, thanks to all the times she'd looked at it, tempted to place the call, then deciding not to. But this time, she grabbed the phone and dialed.

It was time to tell Shane that he was going to be a daddy.

Chapter Five

Shane stood at the mudroom sink, chugging down a large glass of water.

The hay he'd ordered last week had arrived this afternoon, so he'd spent the past couple of hours helping the driver unload a semitruck and trailer. They'd had to stack it in the barn, which meant he'd been bucking bales that weighed ninety pounds or more and stacking them more than chest high.

Needless to say, he'd not only gotten a good workout, but he'd also built up a hearty appetite in the process. So no matter what he decided to fix for dinner, he'd have to make plenty of it. Fortunately, Eva Walker kept a well-stocked pantry and freezer, so he wouldn't have any problem whipping up something good to eat.

For the past week, Shane had been holding down the

fort while Dan, Eva and their four children—two sets of twins, toddlers and second-graders—were in New York, visiting a family friend.

Since Dan had asked him to look after things while he was gone, Shane had packed up his shaving gear and clothes and moved out to the ranch, where he'd spent his days working with the horses and his nights caring for the family menagerie—two dogs, a cat and a hamster.

Shane really didn't mind helping out, since Dan was not only his boss, but his friend. The two of them had met a year or so ago in town at Caroline's Diner, and Dan had offered him a job. Taking the ranch hand position had proved to be a blessing for both of them.

As Shane rinsed his face and hands in the sink, his cell phone rang. He figured it was his nephew calling to arrange the promised day of horseback riding. It had been nearly two months since Shane had agreed to let Evan come out to the ranch, but with school and T-ball schedules, they'd decided to wait until his summer vacation.

Evan was a city kid who would prefer to be a cowboy, if given the chance, and Shane couldn't help but grin at the image of the happy boy in the saddle.

Tempted to let the call roll over to voice mail until he dried his hands and poured himself a glass of iced tea, he glanced at the display, and saw an unfamiliar number. Maybe he'd better not ignore that one. "Hello."

"Shane?"

Jillian? After three months, he'd given up hope of ever hearing her voice again.

"Hey," he said, his heart thudding as though it was clamoring to escape his chest. "How's it going?"

"Good, thanks."

He'd been tempted to contact her again, either by telephone or a drive into the city, but he'd held off. If there was one thing to be said about Shane Hollister, it's that he could be pretty damn stubborn when he put his mind to it.

"How about you?" she asked.

"Not bad."

That same awkward silence filled the line again, so hoping to help things along, he said, "It's good to hear from you."

"Thanks."

Come on, honey, he wanted to say. *Just tell me why you're calling. Are you having a hard time forgetting that night? Or that last kiss?*

He might have nearly written her off, but that didn't mean he no longer thought about her or dreamed about her. Hell, each night he slipped between the sheets of his bed, he'd never been completely alone. Her memory had followed him there.

"I'd like to talk to you," she said. "That is, if you don't mind."

"Not at all. I'm glad you called."

"Actually," she said, "I'd rather talk to you in person. Would it be okay if I drove out to Brighton Valley to see you?"

That was better yet. "Of course. I've got to work most of the day tomorrow, but I'll be finished by late afternoon or early evening." Dan and Eva were due back tomorrow around three, so Shane would take off whenever they arrived.

"Should I drive out to the ranch?"

Shane wasn't so sure that he wanted to have an audience when he and Jillian met—at least, not one that would quiz him after she returned to Houston. But he didn't think it would be a good idea to suggest that she meet him at his place, which was a small studio apartment. It might be too... Well, presumptive, he supposed.

"Why don't we meet in town," he suggested. "There's a great little honky-tonk called the Stagecoach Inn, which is right off the county highway. It shouldn't be too difficult for you to find."

"All right. Can you give me directions?"

"It's pretty easy to spot. If you drive out to Brighton Valley, it's the first thing you'll see when you hit the main drag."

"That sounds easy enough."

Shane wasn't sure why he'd suggested the Stagecoach Inn. He supposed he also wanted to show her a good time—and in a place that was a whole lot different from her usual hangouts.

If she couldn't handle a rip-roaring cowboy bar on a Saturday night, she probably couldn't handle the small-town life in his neck of the woods. And it was best that they found that out early on.

Besides, the music at the Stagecoach Inn was enough to make most people tap their feet and whoop it up. And he hoped to see Jillian let her hair down again.

A couple of months might have passed since he'd

gone to her apartment, but he still thought about her more often than not.

He wished he could say that his interest in her was strictly physical, since there'd been some real chemistry brewing between them. But as the days passed, he'd begun to realize that there was something else drawing him to Jillian's memory, something other than great sex that kept her image fresh in his mind. He actually missed hearing her voice, seeing her smile.

So even if lovemaking wasn't in the cards for them tonight, he was looking forward to whatever time they had.

"When do you want to meet?" he asked.

"I guess it depends on you, since you're the one who has to work tomorrow."

"Then why don't we say five o'clock?" That would give him time to drive home, shower and shave.

"That sounds good."

It certainly did. And since she was going to have a two-hour drive back to Houston, he wondered if she planned to spend the night.

If so, that sounded even better yet.

Jillian entered the Stagecoach Inn more than thirty minutes early—and sporting an unmistakable baby bump. Now that she'd passed her fourth month, her womb seemed to be growing more each day.

Hoping to disguise the evidence of her pregnancy until she had the chance to tell him about it, she'd found a table for two and took a seat that faced the front door. She really hadn't suffered any morning sickness, like other women, but her tummy was tossing and turning now, just at the thought of facing Shane.

She'd been dragging her feet for months, and now that she'd come to tell him, she wished she'd done so sooner. But there wasn't anything she could do about that now.

So, while waiting for him, she scanned the honky-tonk, noting the scuffed and scarred hardwood floor, the red-and-chrome jukebox, the Old-West-style bar that stretched the length of the building. If she'd ever tried to imagine what a cowboy bar would look like, this would be it.

At the table next to hers, two young women wearing tight jeans and scooped-neck T-shirts laughed about something, then clinked their longneck bottles in a toast.

Was this the place where Shane hung out in the evenings or on his days off? Is that why he'd suggested she meet him here?

"Can I get you a drink?" a blond, harried waitress asked.

"Do you have any fruit juice?"

"I'll have to check with the bartender to see what other choices you have, but I know we've got OJ for sure."

"That'll be fine. Thank you."

The bleached-blond waitress had no more than walked away from the table when Jillian's cell phone rang. She grabbed it from her purse, hoping it wasn't Shane telling her he'd been delayed, since she'd put off this conversation for too long as it was.

But when she checked the display, she spotted her grandmother's number.

"Did you get to Brighton Valley safely?" Gram asked.

Jillian pressed her cell phone against her ear, trying to block out the sounds of a Texas two-step as it blasted out of the jukebox. "Yes. It was a pretty easy drive, although it was a long one."

"Where are you?"

"At a bar called the Stagecoach Inn."

"It sounds pretty wild," Gram said. "Are you sure you're okay?"

"I'm fine."

"I don't know about that," Gram said. "I probably should have insisted upon going with you. Where will you be staying?"

"Right next door at the Night Owl Motel."

"That sounds a little...rustic. Don't they have anything nicer than that in town?"

"Not that I know of," Jillian said. "But don't worry. I'll be okay. Besides, you're the one who told me I needed to tell Shane about the baby."

"I know, but..." Gram was clearly having second thoughts.

And so was Jillian. She'd never been in a country bar before, and the Night Owl was a world away from those five-star hotels she'd been used to. But the last thing she wanted to do was to cause her grandmother any undue stress.

"The motel really isn't that bad," she said, trying to talk above a sudden hoot of laughter. "The room is clean, and the bed is soft. I'll be fine tonight. Then I'll drive back to Houston in the morning."

The waitress returned with the orange juice in a Mason jar. "Here you go. Let me know if you'd like anything else."

Jillian offered her a smile. "Thanks. This will be fine for now."

As the waitress walked away, Gram said, "I'm still uneasy about you being there all alone, Jilly."

"Don't be. Shane will be here soon."

"I'm sure he will, but you really don't know him very well."

Oh, for Pete's sake. It was Gram who'd helped her come to the conclusion that she needed to stop procrastinating and tell Shane he was going to be a father. And that wasn't the kind of news to spring on him over the telephone.

"Shane's a nice guy, Gram. You'd like him if you met him. He used to be a police officer, remember?"

"Yes, you mentioned that. But why did he decide to give that job up and go to work on a ranch?"

It probably had something to do with him getting into trouble and being suspended from duty, although Jillian couldn't be sure about that. Last night, on a whim, she'd done a Google search on Shane Hollister and uncovered an online newspaper article about him. From what she'd read, he'd gotten too rough with a man he'd arrested.

Her heart had dropped to the pit of her stomach upon that discovery, especially when she spotted a photograph that convinced her that the men were one and the same.

Just the thought that Shane Hollister, the man who'd loved her with a gentle and expert hand, might harbor a temper or a violent side, set off a wave of nausea. On several occasions, after having too much to drink, Thomas had twisted her arm or given her a shove. So Jillian had kicked herself for not conducting an internet search on Shane sooner.

She'd wanted more details, of course, but short of breaking into police headquarters and hunting for his personnel file, she didn't know how or where to look. But she certainly knew someone who did.

Katie Harris, a journalist who'd been Jillian's college roommate, now worked for a Dallas newspaper. So Jillian had called her and asked her if she could uncover any more information about the incident that had gotten Shane into trouble with the police department.

Katie had been on her way into the office and had called back within an hour. She hadn't found out too much more, other than the fact that Shane had been reinstated to his position with the HPD. But then, a few months later, he'd resigned for no apparent reason.

While tossing and turning in bed last night, Jillian had vacillated on whether to go through with the plan to meet Shane and tell him about the baby, but she'd finally decided to give him the benefit of the doubt.

Of course, she wasn't going to share any of that with her grandmother.

"Well, if you're sure you're okay…" Gram said doubtfully.

"I'll be fine."

"Okay, but call me once you're locked into the motel room for the night."

"I'll do that." Jillian glanced toward the entrance, just in time to see Shane saunter through the door, looking more handsome than a cowboy had a right to. "But I've got to go, Gram. He's here now."

And he'd just spotted her.

When Shane walked into the Stagecoach Inn, he was nearly twenty minutes early. Still, the place was already hopping, even for a Saturday night that was just getting under way. Yet he hadn't gotten two steps inside before he'd spotted Jillian seated at a table for two, looking just as attractive as ever. She was talking on the phone, but as soon as she noticed him, she hung up.

He crossed the scarred oak flooring and made his way to her table. "I see you found the place."

She smiled. "You're right. It was pretty easy, but I have to admit I've never been anywhere like this before."

He figured she meant the honky-tonk, but she could have just as easily been talking about Brighton Valley, as well. "Consider it an adventure."

"I don't know about that. I haven't felt very adventurous lately."

He wondered what she meant by that as he quietly observed her. She wore her platinum-blond hair pulled back today, and a white cotton blouse and black slacks. She'd come looking more casual, more down-to-earth.

More approachable than before, even when he'd found her at home.

As he pulled out the chair next to hers, he asked, "So what are you having? A screwdriver?"

She glanced at her glass, then back at him. "No, it's just orange juice."

The waitress, Trina Shepherd, stopped by the table to ask what he'd like to drink.

After his first visit to the Stagecoach Inn, she'd become a friend of sorts when he'd closed the place down on a slow night. But unlike most guys who'd stayed too long at the bar, he'd been drinking coffee, not throwing back shots.

As a result, Trina knew more about Shane than anyone else in Brighton Valley. But he knew more about her, too.

At one time, before heartache and a few bad choices had left her weathered and worn, she'd been pretty. If a man looked close enough, he could still see hints of it in her eyes.

"Hey," she said, brightening when she spotted Shane. "I haven't seen you in here for a while. How's it going?"

"All right." He tossed her a friendly smile. "How are the kids? Any more broken windows?"

Trina laughed. "There'd better not be. I told them I was going to quit buying groceries if they played dodgeball in the living room again."

Last week, when Shane had stopped by for some hot wings and a beer on his way home, she'd had to leave work to run one of the boys to the E.R. at the Brighton

Valley Medical Center. The kid had nearly cut off his finger trying to clean broken glass off the floor.

Shane introduced the women, calling Jillian a friend of his.

"It's nice to meet you," Trina said to Jillian, before asking Shane, "What can I get you?"

"I'll have a Corona—with lime." He looked at Jillian. "Would you like something stronger than that?"

"No, thanks. I'll stick with juice."

Was she worried that alcohol might lower her inhibitions? She didn't need to be. He'd never take advantage of her, although he supposed she really had no way of knowing that. At least, not yet.

He wouldn't be opposed to taking her back to his place, though. And if she still insisted upon taking things slow, he'd let her have his bed, and he'd sleep on the sofa.

Of course, the night was still young. So who knew how things would end up?

As he cast a glance her way, he saw that she was pulling at the nail on one of her fingers. He couldn't help thinking that she was more nervous than he'd ever seen her.

Why? Was she apprehensive about seeing him again?

If so, was it the honky-tonk setting that was bothering her? Or was it confronting the sexual attraction they'd both found so impossible to ignore?

She stopped messing with her fingernail, then leaned forward and rested her forearms on top of the table. "There's something I need to tell you."

That's what she'd said when she'd called yesterday.

Yet whatever she had to say still seemed to weigh on her mind.

Wanting to make it easier on her, he tossed her a smile. "I hope it's to say that you missed me."

She returned his smile, although hers was laden with whatever had been holding her back. "It's a little more complicated than that."

Apparently so. But her nervousness set him on edge, too.

Finally, she said, "I want you to know that the night we spent in Houston was the first time I'd ever done anything like that."

He'd suspected as much, and a slow grin stretched across his face. "I'm glad to hear it."

So maybe she did have more in mind than a glass of OJ and a chat. He sure hoped so, but he was going to need a little more to go on than that.

Jillian ran her fingertip along the moisture that had gathered on the Mason jar, clearly holding back her announcement.

He couldn't help but chuckle. "Something tells me that it might be easier for you to say what you came to say if you asked Trina to put a little vodka in that glass."

"That wouldn't help." She leaned back in her chair and crossed her arms. "There's no easy way to say this, Shane. I'm pregnant."

Her statement slammed into him like barrage of bullets, making it impossible to speak, let alone react.

Was she suggesting the baby was his? Or had she met someone else in the past few months?

"I thought you should know," she added.

Why? Because the baby *was* his?

They'd used protection... Had they gotten careless that night? Was the condom outdated?

Or had she gotten pregnant by some other guy? Her ex-husband maybe?

Was that why she hadn't contacted him? Was she afraid he wouldn't like the idea of her having some other man's baby?

"How far along are you?" he asked, hoping to do the math and clarify things without asking outright if the baby was his.

"Four and a half months," she said.

That would make it about right.

He supposed there was no way around being direct. "Is it mine?"

She shot him a wounded expression. "Of course it's yours. I told you that I'd never done anything like that before."

Well, how the hell was he supposed to have known that it had to be his? She'd been married up until the time they'd met.... And maybe she'd done it a second or third time—with someone else.

"I know we used a condom," she added, "so I'm not sure how it happened, but it did."

Shane lifted his hat, raked a hand through his hair, then set the Stetson on the table. "I'm sorry, Jillian. I'm just a little...stunned. That's all."

God, he was going to be a father again...

Just the thought caused voice-stealing emotion to

rise in his chest and ball up in his throat—fear and panic, pride...

"I'm not asking for anything," she said. "Like I said before, I plan to raise the baby on my own. And other than the fact that it will probably be a little inconvenient because of school and all, I'm actually looking forward to being a mom. It's just that I thought you should know."

He would have been furious with her if he'd ever found out on his own and learned that she'd kept it from him. But right now, he didn't know quite what to say. His emotions were flying around like stray bullets at a shoot-out—each spinning toward separate targets.

For some reason, thoughts of Marcia came back to taunt him, memories of her taking their toddler and moving out of town. The reminder served to blindside him, making it even more difficult to deal with Jillian's news—and making it way more personal.

"I'm sorry," she said.

"About what?"

"I don't know. Dumping all of this on you, I guess. You must be worried about what this all means, but it doesn't have to mean anything to you. I just thought you should know." She bit down on her bottom lip, her mind undoubtedly going a mile a minute, just as his was doing.

He tried to wrap his mind around the fact that he was going to be a father again, but as he did, thoughts of Joey swept over him: the sight of the newborn coming into the world; that first flutter of a smile; the sight of the chubby baby pulling himself to a stand at the coffee table.

While he should look forward to the idea of having a second chance at fatherhood, the horrendous image of his eighteen-month-old son lying in a small, white, satin-lined casket chased away the sweet memories, and he feared what this might lead to…the anger, the pain, the grief.

After Shane and Marcia had split up, she'd moved out of state, taking Joey with her. Not only had Shane lost out on seeing his son from day to day, he'd been more than five-hundred miles away when he'd received word that he'd…lost him for good.

There was no way Shane wanted to go through that again. And while he had no idea how he would remedy that this time around, he knew he'd have to do something.

He glanced at Jillian, saw her pulling at her fingernail again—clearly worried, nervous and stressed about the situation.

It probably hadn't been easy for her to deliver the news, and he was sorry that his initial reaction had been a little harsh.

"I didn't mean to snap at you," he said, his mind still reeling.

She smiled, then glanced away. "I understand."

But she *didn't;* she *couldn't.*

He probably should tell her about Joey, about how he'd lost his son, about how he still ached with grief. But he didn't think he could open his heart like that without choking up and falling apart.

Besides, the baby news had slammed into him like a runaway train, and it was too soon for him to have a rational reaction to it.

Even if he'd been happy to learn that he was going to be a father again, he wasn't sure if he could trust her. What if Jillian took his baby away and never let him see it again?

He studied her for a moment, watched her slip her hand between the table and her belly, stroking her rounded womb as if caressing the child that grew there.

His child.

Her child.

Fear of repeating the past—the pain, the grief— threatened to suck the breath right out of him, but he couldn't let it. He had to face the truth. He was going to be a father again.

And there was no reason history had to repeat itself.

"When's the baby due?" he asked.

"December third." Her gaze wrapped around his, and she smiled, a whisper of relief chasing away all signs of her nervousness.

How had he missed seeing it before—the obvious pregnancy, the maternal glow?

Jillian might have waited too damn long to tell him about the baby, but he sensed she was happy about the situation.

"Are you planning to drive back to Houston tonight?" he asked.

She caught his gaze. "Actually, I didn't like the idea of being on the road after dark, so I got a room at the Night Owl."

"You could have stayed with me."

"I… Well, I suppose I could have, but I wasn't sure how you'd take the news. And I figured things might be a little awkward between us."

"Maybe so, but we'll need to deal with the situation anyway." And some of it was going to be tough.

Shane scanned the honky-tonk, and when he spotted Trina, he motioned for her to come to the table.

"Are you hungry?" he asked Jillian.

"A little."

When Trina reached the table, Shane said, "We'd like to place an order to go."

"All right. I'll get you a couple of menus." When she returned, she handed each of them the new, one-sided laminated sheet of cardstock that offered a few appetizers and various sandwiches. "I'll give you a chance to look this over, then I'll be back."

"Where are we going?" Jillian asked him.

"When I thought we were just tiptoeing around our attraction and a possible romance, I figured the Stagecoach Inn would be good place to kick up our heels and forget all the reasons why a long-distance relationship wouldn't work out. But now that things have taken an unexpected turn, we need to find a quieter spot so we can talk."

Jillian didn't respond.

Moments later, Trina returned for their orders.

"I'll have the soup and salad combo," Jillian said.

Shane chose the bacon cheeseburger and fries.

"You got it." Trina scratched out their requests on her pad before taking the order to the kitchen.

While Shane and Jillian waited for their food, they made small talk about the music on the jukebox and some of the more interesting characters who had begun to fill the honky-tonk. Yet the tension stretched between them like a worn-out bungee cord ready to snap.

Before long, Trina returned with a take-home bag, as well as the bill. Shane paid the tab, leaving her a generous tip.

"Are you ready?" he asked Jillian, as he scooted back his chair and got to his feet.

Jillian stood and reached for her purse. "So where did you decide to eat?"

"You said you had a room at the Night Owl. Let's go there."

If she had any reservations about taking him back to the motel with her, she didn't say. And Shane was glad. It was important that they take some time to really get to know each other.

And the sooner they got started doing that, the better.

Chapter Six

As dusk settled over Brighton Valley, Shane and Jillian stepped out of the honky-tonk and into the parking lot, which was filling up with a variety of pickups and cars.

"Did you drive from the motel?" he asked.

"No, I walked. The doctor encouraged me to get plenty of exercise, and since I'd been in the car for the past two hours, I thought… Well, it was only a couple of blocks, and it was a good way to stretch my legs."

So she'd already seen a doctor. That was good.

"Is everything going okay?" he asked. "No problems?"

"I had a little nausea at first, but it wasn't anything to complain about."

He was glad to hear that. Marcia had been pretty

sick when she'd been pregnant with Joey, although she felt a bit better by the time she was four or five months along. In fact, if he remembered correctly, Marcia had been at that stage when they'd learned that Joey was going to be a boy.

Shane assumed that, since Jillian was seeing a doctor, she was having all the appropriate tests and exams. So he asked, "Do you know whether it's going to be a girl or a boy?"

"No, I told the doctor I wanted to be surprised." She shrugged. "At least, I'd thought so at the time of my sonogram. But I have to admit, I'm getting more and more curious now."

As they continued walking to the street, their feet crunching along the graveled parking lot, Shane couldn't help stealing a glance at Jillian, checking out the way her belly swelled with their child.

He suspected that she was going to be one of those women who was even more beautiful when she was nine months pregnant. But he didn't want her to think his only concern was the baby, so he asked, "How's school going?"

"It took a little while to get back into the swing of taking notes and studying, but I'm doing okay now. I'm taking two summer courses, and I have finals in two weeks, but nothing too difficult."

"Then what?" he asked.

"I'll begin the student-teaching phase during the fall semester…. Well, that was my game plan before finding out about the baby. It's due right before Christmas, so I'll probably have to wait another semester."

"How are you fixed for money?" he asked.

"I'm okay." She pulled up short. "That's not why I came out here."

He stopped, too. "You need to understand something. I don't expect you to support the baby all by yourself. I'll do my part."

She bit down on her bottom lip, then her gaze lifted and locked on his. Sincerity flared in her eyes, as well as determination. "You don't have to."

Yes, he did.

Unable to help himself, he reached for her hair, touched the silky platinum-blond strands, then let them slip through his fingers. Jillian might be pregnant, and he might have been blown away by the news, but that didn't mean she wasn't a beautiful woman. Or that he'd stopped thinking about wanting to spend another night with her.

Jillian slowly turned away from him, and they continued down the street for two short blocks. Their conversation ceased, as Shane let his thoughts run away with him.

There were a lot of things to consider, a lot yet to be seen. He probably ought to ask more questions. After all, he certainly had plenty of them bouncing around in his head. But he didn't want things to get any heavier between them than they were now.

Not with a lover's moon lighting their path to the motel where she had a room.

The Night Owl, a typical small-town motor inn, sat near the highway, catering to travelers on a budget and to those just passing through. It was the only place to stay on this side of Brighton Valley.

Across town, closer to the thriving community of Wexler, builders and developers had been hard at work, creating several subdivisions along the perimeter of the lake and recreation area.

The Brighton Valley Medical Center, which served the citizens from the entire valley, was located in that part of town, too, as was a supermarket, a department store and a much nicer motel.

But since Shane hadn't wanted to give Jillian any complicated directions, he'd chosen the Stagecoach Inn because it would be easier for her to find. However, he hadn't expected her to need lodging, too. So he should have come up with something closer to Wexler.

He supposed the Night Owl wasn't so bad, even if it wouldn't provide her with the kind of accommodations she was probably used to.

As they approached the single-story building with white stucco walls and a red-tile roof, he spotted a couple of older vehicles in the parking lot, but his gaze lit upon a white, late-model Mercedes coupe in the space closet to number ten, which had to be where they were heading.

Jillian's steps slowed as she reached into her purse, then lifted an old-fashioned key instead of a more modern card and smiled. "I guess this place is in a bit of a time warp."

Her smile suggested she wasn't too bothered by the age of the motel, then she turned and led him to number ten.

Shane was reminded of the last time she'd let him into her hotel room.

As much as he'd like to wrap his arms around her again, kiss her senseless at the door, stretch out naked on the bed and make love until dawn, things were going to be different tonight.

At least, he assumed they would be.

Yet just as before, Shane held the door for Jillian, then followed her inside.

The room, which was clean but sparse, had been simply decorated with a queen-size bed and the typical, nondescript box-style furniture. Again he was reminded that she wasn't used to this kind of lodging, even if she hadn't complained.

He set their bag of food on the small Formica table in the corner, then dug inside for the takeout cartons, plastic utensils and napkins Trina had packed inside.

After setting everything out on the table, he turned to Jillian, intending to follow her lead.

She blushed, and her thick, spiky lashes swept down, then up in a hesitant way.

"What's the matter?"

"I…" She bit down on her bottom lip. "I don't know. I guess I'm just a little concerned about what the future will bring."

For a moment, he wondered if she was talking about them having dinner together in her motel room, while a queen-size bed grew in prominence. But she probably meant the changes the baby would make in their lives, about them trying to be coparents when distance was going to be an issue.

Either way, he didn't like the idea of her being stressed—and not just because she was pregnant. So he stepped forward, cupped her cheeks with both hands and caught her eye. "If you want to know the truth, Jillian, I'm nervous about the future, too. But maybe, if we take the time to get to know each other a whole lot better, things will be easier to deal with."

Her smile, which bordered on pleasure and relief, nearly knocked him to the floor. And he found himself wanting to kiss her in the worst way—and just as he'd done before.

Who was this woman? And what was she doing to him?

Struggling to get his hormones in check, he nodded toward the food on the table. "Why don't we start by having dinner?"

"Okay." She crossed the small room in three steps, then pulled out a chair and took a seat at the table.

He followed her lead, but in spite of suggesting that they eat, he wasn't nearly as hungry as he'd once been. Not for food anyway. But making love had gotten them into this mess in the first place, and doing it again wasn't going to solve any of the problems they now faced.

Instead, it would be imperative to learn more about her.

And one thing that really had him perplexed was her financial situation, since she appeared to be ultra-wealthy, yet lived in a modest apartment.

"You said that you didn't expect any financial support from me. And by the style and make of the car parked outside, as well as those diamond stud earrings you're wearing, I take it money isn't an issue for you."

She lifted the lid to her soup, then reached for a plastic spoon. "I'm afraid things aren't always what they seem. Thanks to a prenuptial agreement, the only things I got from the divorce settlement—besides my freedom—was a modest settlement, my jewelry and the Mercedes you saw out front. But I plan to trade in the car for something more economical in the next couple of weeks. And I've sold some of the jewelry already."

"Then you *do* need money."

"But I don't need *your* money," she insisted. "I didn't come here to secure child support payments. Honestly, Shane, I only came to tell you that you're going to be a father. Just so you'd know. I really wasn't trying to rope you into anything. I can make it on my own."

Shane didn't mean to doubt her. It's just that… Well, he was finding it difficult to get a firm read on her, so he asked, "Then what's the best way for me to help you? I'm afraid the ball is in your court."

Was it?

Jillian had just placed a spoonful of broth into her mouth, so she couldn't have managed a quick response if she'd wanted to, which was just as well. Her first thought was to tell him, *You can stop asking me questions and start answering a few of mine.*

After all, she'd come out to Brighton Valley to learn more about Shane, but she couldn't very well open by bringing up the incident that had caused him to get in trouble with the HPD—even if that was the main thing she both wanted and needed to know.

If she did broach a sticky subject like that right off the bat, he'd wonder how she'd found out about it. And what was she supposed to admit? That she'd not only done an internet search, which everyone did these days, but that she'd also enlisted the help of an investigative journalist?

It was too soon to do that, so she answered as honestly as she could. "I'm really not sure how you can help."

"Like I said before, I want to be involved in the baby's life."

"Well, under the circumstances, that's going to be a little tough, isn't it?"

It was the truth, although she hoped the words didn't come across as harshly as they sounded after the fact.

Shane glanced down at his uneaten burger, then met her gaze. Yet he didn't speak.

He was a handsome man and a good lover—that, she knew. But she had no idea what was under the surface—or what kind of father he'd make. And his desire to be a part of the baby's life caught her off guard, causing her maternal instincts to kick in.

"If you're thinking you'd like to share custody, that won't work. A baby needs its mother."

Shane stiffened as if she'd struck him, and she wasn't sure why. He lived two hours away. How could they possibly consider joint custody until the child was older? And even then, she wasn't willing to enter an arrangement like that until she knew him better and could determine whether he harbored either a short fuse or a violent streak.

She placed the lid back on her soup container, no longer hungry. Why had she told him she was pregnant? Okay, so it wouldn't have been right to keep it from him, but she was having serious misgivings.

Shane pushed his food aside. "Look, I didn't mean that I expected to have the baby every other weekend, it's just that... Well, I have a big family and a lot of nieces and nephews. I want them to know my son and to be able to play with him."

"Your *son?*" She smiled, assuming that he probably thought he could relate better to a boy—playing ball, riding horses and whatever activities daddies liked to do with their children. "What if the baby is a girl?"

He paused, and that fleeting shadow darkened his eyes again, moving on as quickly as it had arisen.

"A little girl would be fine with me," he said. "I'm just trying to figure out how to make a difficult situation work out for everyone involved."

"Everyone?"

"You, me *and* the baby."

Jillian thought about that for a moment, then decided that he wasn't being completely unreasonable. "I suppose you could drive to Houston on the weekends and visit us."

Again, he stiffened, as if offended by the offer.

"I'd also be happy to invite your nieces and nephews over to spend time with their new cousin," she added.

He seemed to be mulling that over. Couldn't he see that she was willing to compromise—when possible?

She reached across the table and placed her hand on his forearm, felt the strength of well-defined muscles.

"I'm sure you're a wonderful man, Shane. And that you'll make a great father. It's just that…I don't really know that yet. I don't know much about you. I'm sorry if I'm coming across as resistant or difficult. My motherly instincts must be coming into play."

At that, she could feel the tension ease in his forearm, and his expression softened.

"I already made a mistake by marrying a man I couldn't trust," she said. "So I hope you won't blame me for being gun-shy when it comes to jumping into any kind of relationship, especially when I have a baby to consider this time around."

He placed his hand on top of hers, his touch sending a whisper of heat coursing through her.

Yet it was the intensity of his gaze, the ragged sincerity in his eyes, that urged her to give him a chance—to give them *all* one.

"I can't blame you for wanting to be careful," he said. "I'm a little gun-shy, too. And since you're going to be the mother of my baby, I'd like to know with absolute certainty that you'll make a good one."

She hadn't realized that he had some of the same concerns that she had, a thought that soared crazily like a broken kite on a snapped string.

"You could be a good actress," he said, "but something tells me that you're every bit the woman I thought you were when I showed up at your house in Houston, hoping a long-distance relationship might work out between us. But back then, I figured it was worth the risk of striking out if you'd rejected the idea."

"And *now?*"

"With a baby in the balance, I think it's critical for us to know the truth about each other."

She couldn't agree more.

After a beat, she asked, "So now what? Where do we go from here?"

She expected his gaze to travel to the bed in the center of the room. After all, that's where they knew each other best. But instead, he focused on her, this time turning her heart inside out.

"You mentioned that your fall semester will be starting," he said.

"Yes, in three weeks." She'd also planned to take a class through the local YMCA on newborn and infant development in the evenings. And she hoped to start preparing a nursery.

He leaned forward, his hand still lightly pressing on hers. "Why don't you come out to Brighton Valley while you're still out of school? I'll cut back on my hours at the ranch, and we can use the time to get to know each other better."

The invitation took her aback, yet she thought long and hard over what he was proposing.

Where would she stay? Even a room at the Night Owl would get expensive after a while. She'd been trying to stretch her dollars so that her money would last until she secured a teaching position and could afford day care.

As if reading her mind, he said, "You can stay in my apartment with me. I'll sleep on the sofa—if you're worried about my motives."

She wasn't sure how she felt about any of what he

was suggesting, but they did need time to get to know each other. And staying with him seemed like a logical plan, at least, financially speaking.

"All right," she said. "I'll come to Brighton Valley for a couple of weeks. And I'll stay with you."

He sat back in his seat, his eyes growing bright. "I think you've made a good decision."

She wasn't so sure about that.

Staying with him could make things a lot more complicated than they were right now.

Especially since she wasn't excited about him sleeping on the sofa when she knew how much she'd once enjoyed having him in her bed.

Two weeks later, after paying the woman who'd scrubbed his apartment from top to bottom and sending her on her way, Shane stood in the living room, surveying the results of her efforts and breathing in the scent of lemon oil and various cleaning products.

It's not as though he was a slob, but he wanted Jillian to be comfortable while she stayed with him. Of course, he had no idea how she might feel about him living in an apartment over Caroline's Diner.

When Shane had first come to Brighton Valley, he'd stopped for lunch at the small-town restaurant, where he'd had the best chicken and dumplings he'd ever eaten. His waitress had asked if he was new in town, and when he'd nodded, she'd told him about the vacancy upstairs. So after meeting Dan Walker and landing a job as a ranch hand that very same day, he'd realized that his luck had finally begun to turn.

Dan had also told him he could stay in the bunk-house, but while Shane had appreciated the offer, he'd graciously declined. He preferred having a place of his own, where he could hang his hat and escape after a hard day's labor.

And so he'd set about making his new digs feel like home, adding a few pieces of furniture now and then, as well as a flat-screen television and a state-of-the-art sound system. He might not spend very much time at home, but when he did, he wanted a few comforts.

Hopefully, Jillian would find the apartment appealing, as well. After all, she'd be living here for the next two weeks.

Shane crossed the floor to the kitchen, where the sink, countertops and appliances all sparkled. Then he opened the fridge, which he'd stocked with food and drinks after a run to the market last night. Jillian would have plenty of stuff to choose from, including fresh fruits and vegetables.

Now all he had to do was wait for her to arrive.

After closing the refrigerator, he strode to the window and peered into the street, expecting her to arrive soon—unless she'd gotten lost along the way.

He was really looking forward to seeing her again, although he felt badly about leaving Dan Walker in a lurch for the next week. But Dan was a family man and understood the situation, once Shane had explained the surprising predicament he'd found himself in. Dan had listened, then insisted that he'd be able to handle things on his own.

Shane planned to take off only the first week of Jillian's visit. He would spend as much time with her as he could for those seven days. After that, she'd need to keep herself busy during the day. It shouldn't be too difficult. There were stores along Main, if she felt like shopping. She could even visit Darla's Salon. And there was a library in Wexler, which wasn't too far away.

He still couldn't believe that she'd gotten pregnant on their one and only night together. Yet the more he thought about it, the better he felt about it.

It didn't seem fair, though. After his divorce, he'd sworn off women who wanted different things out of life than he did. But now he'd gotten involved with another one, a woman who'd set her sights on things outside his world.

Of course, that might change with time. He had a week or two to tempt Jillian with everything a small town like Brighton Valley had to offer, although something told him it wouldn't be good enough for her.

As it neared five o'clock, the time she was due to arrive, Shane went downstairs to sit on the green wrought-iron bench in front of the diner.

He didn't have to wait long. Moments later she arrived driving a silver Honda Accord. Apparently she'd gotten rid of the Mercedes, just as she'd told him.

As she climbed out of the driver's seat, he took note of her casual clothing—jeans, a white fitted top that stretched over her baby bump and a lightweight chambray shirt.

Her hair hung to her shoulders in a loose, carefree style, reminding him of the way it had looked splayed on a pillow and the way those silky strands had felt as they'd slipped through his fingers that same night.

He was sorely tempted to greet her with a hug, but he got to his feet and shoved his hands into the front pockets of his jeans instead. No need to come on too strong, he supposed.

"Did you have any trouble finding the place?" he asked.

"No, it was pretty easy." She cast him a smile that seemed almost waifish and lost, then opened the rear passenger door for her suitcase.

"I'll get that for you," he said, stepping forward and catching an amazing whiff of her scent—something lilac, he guessed.

She thanked him, then allowed him to reach into the car. After he snatched her bag and closed the door, she hit the lock button on the key remote.

"Come on," he said, "I'll show you where I live."

He led her up the narrow stairway between the diner and the drugstore.

Once they were upstairs, he opened the door, then stepped aside and let her enter first.

As she scanned the living room, he tried to see the place from her perspective. Would she be comfortable here? Would she find it too modest, too humble?

"It's not much," he said, "but it's home."

She didn't respond, which made him wonder if she found it lacking in some way. Then she crossed the hardwood floor to the window that looked out into the street.

When she turned around, she smiled, lighting up the

room in an unexpected way. "When you said you lived in an apartment, I thought it would be in a typical complex, like mine. I didn't expect something like this."

Was that good or bad?

He supposed it shouldn't matter, yet it did. "So what do you think?"

"It's got an interesting view." She walked to the sofa, which he'd purchased a couple of months ago, and placed her hand along the backrest. "I like it."

Thank goodness. It would have been tough if she were to hate the idea of being stuck here for a couple of weeks. So he returned her smile, then nodded toward the bedroom. "I'll show you where you can put your things."

"All right."

As he led her through the doorway, he said, "I made some space for you in the closet, so you can hang up some of your clothes, if you want to. And I emptied the top two drawers of the dresser. I hope that'll give you enough room."

He'd also made sure there was a brand-new tube of toothpaste for her to use, and he'd purchased two fluffy white towels, which now hung pristinely on the rack.

"I didn't expect you to go to any trouble for me," she said.

"It was no trouble." He placed her suitcase on the bed. "If you need some time to rest or settle in, I can make myself scarce. Or if you want something to eat, we can go down to the diner. I've got plenty of food in the fridge, but to tell you the truth, I eat most of my meals at Caroline's."

"It's so close. I can see where it would be easier for you."

"Yeah, but Caroline's also one heck of a cook." He chuckled. "I'd never want my mom to know this, but some of the meals at the diner are actually tastier than the ones I get when I'm back home."

Jillian smiled. "I'd like to check out Caroline's cooking and see if it holds up to my grandmother's."

Ten minutes later, after Jillian had settled in, Shane took her to the diner, where she scanned the interior, clearly taking in the white café-style curtains on the front windows, the yellow walls with a wallpaper border, as well as the wooden tables and chairs.

"It sure looks like a down-home-style restaurant," she said as she glanced at the chalkboard that advertised a full meal for seven dollars and ninety-nine cents.

In bright yellow chalk on black, someone had written, *What the Sheriff Ate,* followed by, *Meat Loaf, Green Beans w/ Almonds, Mashed Potatoes and Peach Cobbler.*

"What does that mean?" Jillian asked.

"Caroline's married to the town sheriff, so that's how she lists the daily special."

Jillian smiled. "That's really cute. And that meat loaf plate sounds good to me, especially with the peach cobbler."

"Then let's find a place to sit."

Shane and Jillian had no more taken seats at an empty table when he saw Sam Jennings enter the café. In his early sixties, with silver hair and a barrel chest, the Brighton Valley sheriff also had a belly that lapped over his belt, thanks to nearly forty years of his wife's cooking.

Sam waved at Shane, then headed for the table. The two men had become friends a while back, after a rash of robberies in town had left the sheriff perplexed. Shane had offered his help by studying the crime scene evidence, and they'd soon found the culprit, who was now behind bars.

"How's it going?" Sam asked.

"Great." Shane introduced the jovial sheriff to Jillian.

After the customary greetings, Sam stuck around and chatted for a while, mostly about the weather, the fact that the bass were really biting down at the lake and that Charlie Boswell, who'd just retired as fire chief, planned to take his wife on an Alaskan cruise.

Shane hoped Jillian didn't mind the small-town talk. When he glanced across the table at her, she was smiling, which suggested she was okay with it all.

So far, so good, he thought.

As Sam made his way to one of the booths at the back of the diner to join another Brighton Valley old-timer, Margie, the waitress, stopped by the table with menus and two glasses of water.

"We won't need to look at these," Shane said, handing the menus back. "We'd each like the special."

Margie didn't bother taking out her notepad. "You won't be sorry. Those green beans are really fresh. So what would you like to drink?"

"I'll have seltzer," Jillian said.

Margie looked at Shane and smiled. "How about you, cowboy?"

"Iced tea."

"You got it." Margie started to walk away, then stopped. "Say, how are things going out at the ranch? I heard one of Dan and Eva's twins came down with strep throat."

"That was Kevin," Shane said. "But he's feeling a lot better now. Fortunately, he didn't share his germs with the rest of the family."

"I'm glad to hear that," Margie said before walking back to the kitchen with their orders.

"I take it she was talking about your boss and his kids," Jillian said.

"Yep. Dan and Eva have two sets of twins. I'll probably take you out to meet them while you're here."

"I'd like that."

She would? Shane took that to be another good sign that she didn't find Brighton Valley to be a hick town or a total waste of her vacation time.

"I'm wondering, though. How do your friends feel about our living arrangement? What did you tell them about me?"

"Dan and Eva are two of the nicest people you'll meet. I told them the truth—that we met in Houston, that we conceived a child and that we need to sort through some things. They actually asked me to bring you out to the ranch."

She bit down on her bottom lip, then surveyed the diner. When her gaze returned to his, she gave a little shrug. "But what about everyone else in town? They all seem to know each other—and what's going on in their lives. What have you told them about me?"

"Just that we're friends. It's really none of their business."

As she reached for her glass and took a sip of water, he wondered if she was concerned about being fodder for gossip.

He supposed there were some people who might find her condition and her presence in town worthy of discussion, but there wasn't much he could do about it.

Opting to change the subject and to get her mind off the small-town rumor mill, he asked, "Have you ever been on a ranch before?"

"No, so it ought to be interesting. I'd also like to see where you work."

It was another way to get to know him better, he supposed. He couldn't blame her for that.

He leaned forward and placed his elbows on the table. "I've got an idea. After dinner, let's take a walk."

"All right, but where?"

"Just outside the diner. We can check out some of the shops on Main Street. I think you'd enjoy that. You might also be surprised at how much fun it is to people watch in this town."

Jillian blessed him with a pretty smile. "That sounds great."

It did? That was better news yet, especially since Shane planned to convince Jillian that Brighton Valley wasn't just a little Podunk town.

And that it would be an ideal place to raise their child.

Chapter Seven

Jillian and Shane spent the evening window shopping along the main drag of Brighton Valley. Along the way, she'd also met some of the more colorful citizens who called the small town home, like Anson Pratt, who sat outside the drugstore, whittling small wooden animals to give to the kids in the pediatric ward at Brighton Valley Medical Center.

On several occasions, her shoulder had brushed against Shane's. Each time it happened, she'd been tempted to slip her hand into his.

She'd been alone for months, determined to create a home for her baby while she chased her dream to teach. And now, as she strolled along one of Brighton Valley's quaint, tree-shaded streets, she relished Shane's musky scent and the soul-stirring sound of his soft Southern drawl.

With each step they took, the memory of their lovemaking grew stronger, triggering an almost overwhelming sense of sexual awareness and urging her to reach out to him, to take whatever he had to offer.

Instead, she continued to walk by his side, convinced that she needed to fight temptation. After all, she might want to pin her hopes on him as her lover and her baby's father, but it was way too soon for that.

What if it was all an act? What if he was only playing the part of a nice guy?

It was a risk she wasn't willing to take this early in the game.

Yet that didn't mean she wasn't enjoying their evening as they toured the shops, chatting about things as Shane gave her his tour. She'd especially found it interesting to learn that Darla Ortiz, who owned the hair salon, had been a Hollywood actress back in the day.

"Darla has a wall full of framed, black-and-white head shots of various movie stars who were popular forty and fifty years ago," Shane said, "and each one is autographed to her."

"That's so cool! I'll have to make an appointment while I'm here, just so I can see those photos."

"Do you like old movies?" he asked, as if he'd just uncovered an interesting bit of Jillian trivia.

"My grandparents raised me, remember? So I spent a lot of time watching the classics on television."

He grew pensive for a moment, then turned to her and brightened. "If you don't mind spending a quiet evening at home, I can see if there are any good movies on TV."

"Sure. That sounds good to me."

Once they were back at the apartment, Shane reached for the remote and clicked on the television. Then he surfed the channels, pausing momentarily to catch a baseball score.

"I'm not finding anything too exciting," he said, "but there's an old Cary Grant movie that will be starting in a couple of minutes. Are you up for something like that?"

"Which one is it?"

"*Father Goose,* with Leslie Caron."

"Ooh, that's a good one."

"You don't mind seeing it again?"

"Not at all."

Jillian wasn't sure how Shane actually felt about spending the evening watching classic movies, especially one he might consider a chick flick, but she'd find out soon enough.

After placing the television remote on the glass-topped coffee table, Shane went into the kitchen. A few minutes later, the microwave hummed. Before long, a popping sound let her know that he was making popcorn. She smiled at the thoughtful gesture.

"I'm going to make a root beer float," he called, as he opened the freezer door. "Would you like one, too? I can also give you plain ice cream or something else to drink."

"Are you kidding? I'd love one. I haven't had a float since my grandfather died. Do you need some help?"

"Nope. I've got it."

As the movie began, they took seats on the sofa, with the bowl of popcorn between them and root beer floats in hand, and soon fell into the story.

Shane laughed in all the appropriate spots, which Jillian took to mean that he found the old movie as entertaining as she did. But even if that wasn't the case, she had to give him credit for being a good sport.

The film was a classic romantic comedy at its best, and as Jillian reached into the popcorn bowl, her fingers brushed Shane's, sending a rush of heat up her arm.

As she glanced at him, she caught him looking at her.

For a moment, the only romance she could think about was the one brewing between her and Shane, especially since it was nearing the witching hour for lovers.

Not midnight, of course, but bedtime…

"Sorry," she said, conjuring up an unaffected smile.

"No problem."

As their gazes locked, as the sexual awareness that buzzed between them grew almost deafening, she broke eye contact and returned her focus to the television screen. Yet even though she pretended to watch Cary and Leslie with the interest of an avid fan, it took ages to get back into the story.

When the credits began to roll on the screen, Shane got to his feet. "Are you up for another movie? Or maybe a game of cards?"

She smiled, realizing the next two weeks might

prove to be more pleasant than either of them had thought.

"Actually," she admitted, "I didn't sleep very well last night, and I'm fading fast."

"All right. You take the room. I'll fix a bed on the sofa."

While she was tempted to object and tell him that she didn't mind sharing the bed with him, she wasn't sure she would be able to climb between the sheets and face the wall when he was just an arm's reach away. So she clamped her mouth shut and watched him pull a blanket and pillow out of the linen closet.

"You can have the bathroom first," he said. "I'll use it when you're finished."

"I won't be long." As she headed for the bedroom to get her makeup bag and nightgown, she realized she ought to be grateful for Shane's concessions and his obvious attempt to make her feel welcome and at home.

But for some reason, as she prepared for bed, disappointment settled over her at the thought of sleeping alone.

Jillian might have turned in early last night, but she'd lain in bed for hours, unable to sleep.

Just knowing that Shane was mere steps away had driven her crazy, and the fact that he'd been so sweet to her had only made it worse. He'd treated her with nothing but kindness and respect ever since the night they'd first met, and it was difficult to imagine him as a police officer who'd overstepped his bounds and assaulted a suspect in custody.

Of course, she didn't know that he'd done anything wrong. After all, the article she'd read said that he'd been reinstated. So that probably meant he'd been innocent of any wrongdoing.

She'd been tempted to bring it up, to ask him about it, but she'd decided to wait for her friend to report back with more details. Then she could come to her own conclusions about the man who'd shown her only kindness and understanding.

Or was she missing something?

In spite of him having a gentle side, did he resort to violence when frustrated, angry or provoked?

Thomas had on occasion, and it had been a little frightening. So even though Jillian found it hard to believe that Shane had a similar trait, the question was too important to ignore. Yet by the time she'd fallen asleep at two in the morning, she hadn't been any closer to having an answer.

And now, as she threw off the covers and rolled out of bed, she glanced at the clock on the bureau, only to realize it was after eight. So she slipped on her robe and padded into the living area.

The aroma of brewing coffee and sizzling bacon filled the air, taunting her taste buds. But that was nothing compared with the stirring ache of hunger she felt at seeing Shane move about the small kitchen, balancing his time between the skillet of breakfast meat and a mixing bowl into which he was cracking an egg.

Thomas wouldn't have been caught dead in a kitchen, let alone cooking. But then again, he'd grown up with a full household staff that had been quick to handle his every need.

Jillian placed a hand on her growing tummy and caressed the swell of her womb. If she and Shane ended up with a shared-custody arrangement, would he go to this kind of trouble for their child? She hoped so.

Before she could utter a cheerful, "Good morning," she watched him grimace and stroke the back of his neck, kneading the muscles from the top to the bottom.

"What's the matter?" she asked.

He turned, clearly not aware that she'd been watching him, then his hand lowered and a smile burst across his freshly shaven face. "Hey! Good morning."

"You were rubbing your neck. Does it hurt?"

"It's not that bad. I just slept on it wrong."

She wasn't exactly buying that, since he'd probably been cramped on the sofa and hadn't been able to stretch out all the way.

"I'm sorry," she said.

"About what?"

"Not letting you have the bed."

"Don't give it another thought. I fall asleep watching TV all the time, so when I bought that sofa, I made sure it was comfortable."

Yes, but would it have hurt to let him stretch out on the bed beside her? Sleeping together didn't mean they had to have sex.

Had to?

Yeah, right. Making love with Shane Hollister would be a privilege, not a chore.

As the sweet memories of their one night together

rose to the surface, tempting her, taunting her, she tamped them down the best she could. Those were dangerous thoughts for a woman who didn't want their relationship to be complicated.

Maybe she should just wait and see what the day would bring.

"I'm making hotcakes and bacon for breakfast," Shane said, turning back to his work. "I hope that's okay. I also have cereal in the pantry and yogurt in the fridge—if you'd rather have something else."

To be honest, she would prefer to eat something lighter than pancakes, something with fewer carbs and less sugar. But how could she tell him that when he'd tried so hard to surprise her this morning?

So she said, "Hotcakes sound great. I'll have cereal and fruit tomorrow morning."

"All right." He turned the fire down on the bacon, then reached into a drawer for the egg beaters. "Would you like some coffee?"

"I've cut back on caffeine, so I'll just have a glass of orange juice, if that's okay."

"Of course. It's in the fridge."

She made her way to the kitchen area, opened the refrigerator and scanned the full shelves until she found a carton of OJ.

"You know," Shane said, while she carried the juice to the counter and reached for a glass. "I was thinking about something that might be fun to do today. How would you like to ride out to the lake? We could pack a lunch, maybe do some fishing."

"Sure." She'd had a good time when they'd strolled

down Main Street last night. And being outdoors on such a lovely summer day was very appealing.

As she poured the juice, she asked, "Do I have time to shower before breakfast? I'll make it quick."

"Take your time. I can keep everything warm."

Less than an hour later, after they'd eaten breakfast and made a lunch of turkey sandwiches, grapes, chips and bottled water, they climbed into Shane's pickup and drove across town to the lake.

On the way, Shane pointed out the Brighton Valley Medical Center, as well as the new elementary school.

"The older kids have had to take the bus to Wexler for years," he said, "but that'll soon be a thing of the past. They're going to build a new high school next year."

Jillian nodded, as though he was just making casual conversation, but from the way he was singing the praises of Brighton Valley, she began to wonder if he was trying to sell her on the place.

She almost discarded the idea, then thought better of it.

Was that what he was trying to do? She had a feeling it was.

She stole a glance across the seat at the handsome cowboy's profile, which was enough to turn a woman's heart on end.

With an elbow resting on the open window, one hand on the wheel, his eyes on the road ahead and a boyish grin on his face, he didn't seem to be plotting and planning.

So she turned back to studying the passing scenery, the landscape and buildings.

Sure, the town was quaint and the people she'd met so far seemed nice. It was the kind of place she wouldn't mind visiting. But Jillian wouldn't want to move here. After all, her grandmother lived in Houston. And that's where the university was located.

It was one thing to take off a semester because she was due to have a baby, but there's no way she'd give up her plan to get a credential or her dream of teaching. Not again.

And there was no way she'd ever leave Gram all alone in the city, without any family nearby.

"Is there any chance you'd move back to Houston?" she asked.

"No, not at this point in my life."

"Why not?"

He paused for a moment, and she assumed he might be planning to sing the praises of small-town life. Instead, he said, "It's complicated."

She wondered if his move had anything to do with the reason he'd left the HPD, but his short, clipped answer was proof that he didn't want to discuss the details with her.

If that was the case, she'd let the subject drop for a while, but that didn't mean she wouldn't get the answer to her question, even if she had to draw it out of him— one word at a time.

After Shane parked in the graveled lot by the lake, he left the cooler with their lunch locked in his pickup, then took Jillian on a leisurely walk along one of the many hiking trails.

"It's really pretty out here," she said. "I'm glad you suggested we spend the day at the lake."

"I thought you'd like it." If truth be told, he hoped that she would see that Brighton Valley had a lot to offer her and the baby. Otherwise, Shane had no idea how he'd ever be able to establish a relationship with his son or daughter.

He might not have embraced the news when she'd first told him she was pregnant, and he might be afraid of what the future would bring, but if he was going to be a father, he wanted to be a part of his child's life.

When they reached the end of one trail and started toward the lakeshore, he suggested that they find a place to sit for a while. "We can watch people launch their boats and cast their lines. What do you think?"

"I'm game if you are."

They walked several yards across the lawn to a shady spot under a maple tree.

"How's this?" Shane asked. "Do you mind sitting on the grass?"

"Not at all." As she knelt down and took a seat, Shane sat beside her, tempted to stretch out instead.

"There's nothing better than a day spent fishing," he said.

Jillian smiled, her blue eyes as bright as the summer sky overhead. "My grandpa would have agreed with you. When he was alive, he loved to fish, and once in a while, he'd even take me along. But I think he actually preferred going out by himself. He used to say that it gave him time to commune with nature and to talk to God."

"I like being outdoors for the very same reason, although I haven't fished since I was in my late teens. Maybe that's why I enjoy working on the ranch. I love the fresh air, the sunshine."

"Is that why you moved from the city?"

"That's part of it." Unwilling to give her a opening to quiz him about his other reasons, he added, "This is a great place to live."

She rested her hand along the top of her pregnant belly. "Some people might argue with you there."

Was she talking about herself?

Probably.

"I guess there are those who like more glitz and glamour in their lives," he said. "More culture."

She seemed to ponder his comment a moment. "I had that kind of life once, and for the most part, it was nice while it lasted. But I gave it all up without any reservations so I wouldn't have to deal with Thomas's lies and infidelity."

Shane could understand that.

"I'm the first and only one in the Hollister family to get a divorce," he admitted, "so it wasn't easy when Marcia and I finally decided to call it quits. But sometimes two pleasant and personable people make a lousy couple."

He tossed a casual glance Jillian's way, saw her leaning back in a relaxed pose, their baby front and center.

When she caught his gaze, he said, "You know what I mean?"

She nodded.

"I was a far cry from the perfect husband," he added. "And the men in my family have always had a tendency to raise their voices when angry. But I wouldn't have cheated."

Her brow knit, as though she wasn't sure if she believed him. Or maybe she was just giving his revelation some thought. After all, he hadn't shared the details of his divorce with her before, although he was glad he finally had.

Still, he thought it was a good idea to add, "When I make a vow or give my word, it means something."

She looked out at the lake for a moment, then turned her attention back to him. "I'm glad to hear that. My mom never married my dad, but my grandparents taught me the meaning of love, commitment and family. It was a painful eye-opener to learn that not everyone is able to keep that kind of promise to a spouse."

"I guess, in a sense, we were both disillusioned by someone we considered a lifetime partner."

A pair of mallard ducks—one male, the other female—quacked as they flew overhead, then landed on the water.

"In your case," Jillian began, "who filed for divorce?"

He wasn't sure why that mattered to her. Maybe because she was trying to determine if he was a quitter.

He wasn't, although there were a few people in his family who never understood why he'd walked away from the HPD. But he'd had his reasons.

"My wife was the one who filed, although, by that time, I was ready to throw in the towel, too."

Shane studied the ducks, wondering if the feathered mates had as much trouble getting along and sticking together as some humans did.

"Did your ex-wife ever remarry?"

"Yes, she did. And I think she's better off now. She found someone who was more her style. He also has a nine-to-five job that's safe."

"I can see where she'd worry about you while you were out on patrol."

Shane tensed for a moment, remembering the unfounded accusations Marcia had often thrown at him, then chuffed. "I think her biggest fear was that I was away from home so much, that I would screw around on her."

"And you honestly didn't cheat?"

He'd already told her that he hadn't, but since her faith in the male species had been seriously undermined, thanks to the jerk she'd married, Shane didn't take offense when she challenged his honesty.

"No," he said, "I didn't cheat."

Okay, so his tone had betrayed him. He *had* been a little offended, after all.

"I'm sorry," she said. "I didn't mean to imply you weren't telling me the truth."

"I guess that's the result of having a spouse lie and cheat." He removed his Stetson and placed it on the grass beside him. "For what it's worth, I don't plan to make any of the same mistakes again, either. If I ever remarry, it'll be to a woman who's happy with my line of work, whatever that is."

"Does that mean you don't plan to be a cowboy the rest of your life?"

"I'm not sure. But that's not the point. I think couples need to be a team."

"I agree."

They continued to sit there, locked in silence. Then she turned again. This time her knee brushed his— taunting him with her touch, with her nearness.

"Do you think you'll *ever* move back to Houston?" she asked.

"Only for visits. Sometimes I miss my job. I was very good at what I did. But I'm happy with my life here. Things are more laid-back, more real."

As the silence stretched between them again, Shane glanced at his watch and noted the time.

"Are you ready for lunch?" he asked.

"Actually, I *am* getting a little hungry."

"Then let's go." He grabbed his hat, got to his feet, then reached out to help her up.

The feel of her hand in his was enough to make him rethink his stance about living in Brighton Valley permanently—if it meant a relationship was completely out of the question. There was something about Jillian that made him wonder if things could be different, that made him *want* them to be.

As they headed back to the parking lot to get the cooler, they approached the playground, where several local families had gathered to spend a few hours with their kids.

They'd yet to pass by it when Jillian reached for Shane's arm and pulled him to a stop. Her fingers gripped his flesh—not hard—but with enough emotion to cause his blood to warm and his heart to race.

When he turned toward her, their gazes locked.

"Let's watch the kids play for a while," she said. "Do you mind?"

Yeah, he minded. The last time he'd been with Joey, he'd driven to Marcia's house and got to spend the afternoon with him. They'd gone to get lunch at McDonald's, then to the park.

But if spending time by the playground convinced Jillian that she'd like to bring their baby here to play in the sand or on the swing set, then he'd agree.

He nodded toward an empty bench. "There's a place to sit over there."

After they'd settled into their seats, Jillian pointed to a mommy showing her preschool-age girl how to blow dandelion seeds in the air. "Isn't that sweet?"

But Shane's gaze went beyond the woman and child to the daddy helping his chubby-legged toddler climb the slide, taking care to follow the boy up each step.

He turned his face away, looking for a bird, a tree, a rock—anything that he could focus on so she wouldn't see the crushing grief in his eyes.

"Is something wrong?" she asked.

Would Jillian understand if he told her about Joey, about how he'd died? How Shane had blamed himself somehow, even though he hadn't been in the car that day, hadn't been the one behind the wheel?

She reached out and touched his hand, sending a warm, healing balm to his bones.

"I…uh…" He cleared his throat, yet his voice retained a husky tone. "My wife and I had a son. A baby boy."

Her fingers probed deeper on his hand, gentle but firm. "What happened?"

"He…was killed in a car accident." Shane cleared his throat again, yet he couldn't seem to shake the rusty, cracked sound in his voice. "My, uh…his mother was driving, and Joey was in the car seat in back when she hit a patch of ice and fishtailed into the path of a semi-truck."

"I'm so sorry, Shane," Jillian said softly. "I don't know what to say."

"I…" He cleared his throat for a third time. "I took it pretty hard."

"I can't even imagine what you've been through."

"Yeah. It was tough." He blew out a tattered sigh. "And I wish that I would have handled it differently."

She brushed her thumb across the top of his hand, grazing the skin near his wrist as if trying to offer what little comfort she could.

"I'd expected the overwhelming pain and sadness," he said, "but I hadn't been prepared for the anger."

"I think that's only natural. And part of the grieving process."

He shrugged. "I was upset with my ex-wife and said some things I shouldn't have. She was devastated by Joey's death, too, and didn't need me to lash out at her like I did."

"People say things when they're hurting that they don't always mean."

"That's the problem. I meant them. And I still do. I just wish I hadn't said anything out loud."

"What did you say?"

"I resented her for moving out, for not trying to make the marriage work for Joey's sake. And when he died, I blamed her, saying it was all her fault. And not just because she'd been driving the car, but because she'd taken him away from me, and I'd missed out on the last three months of his life."

He turned his hand to the side, taking hers with it and clutching her in a warm, desperate grip. "I'm sorry for rambling."

Her words came out in a soft whisper. "You didn't ramble."

"Yeah, well, I don't usually talk about it."

"Maybe you should."

"You might be right."

Yet even though he'd finally said it, Jillian didn't leave it alone. "How long has it been?"

"About a year ago. It's still hard."

"How long have you and his mother been divorced?"

"It's been final for about five months. Joey's death sort of slowed the legal process. Neither one of us was really able to deal with anything for a while."

Jillian didn't say a word. Instead, she continued to hold his hand, to offer comfort. And for a moment, he accepted it.

She might sympathize with him, but she'd never

understand what he'd dealt with, thanks to Marcia's refusal to compromise.

Did she realize that now, after spilling his guts, that he feared grieving for two children—a son he'd lost through death and a baby he'd yet to meet?

What if Jillian refused to let him be a part of their son or daughter's life? What if she, like Marcia, hooked up with someone else and moved away?

As unsettling as that thought was, he couldn't help but think that Jillian would probably be better off with a guy who could provide all the nicer things in life—a guy who wasn't a cowboy *or* a cop. And that fact didn't sit any better.

After all, Jillian had said the same thing Marcia had once told him. *Babies belong with their mothers.*

All right. Maybe they did. That's the reason he'd stood by and watched Marcia take Joey from him in the first place.

What would stop Jillian from doing the same thing?

Was it any wonder he was torn between insisting that Jillian let him be a part of the new baby's life and letting go before his heart had the chance to break all over again?

Chapter Eight

As Jillian listened to Shane's heartfelt disclosure and gazed into his watery eyes, something frail and broken peered out at her, clenching her heart.

A wave of sympathy surged from her womb to her throat, making it difficult to breathe, let alone respond. So she took his hand, trying to connect with him on some level, trying to ease his pain.

He wrapped his fingers around hers, clutching her in a warm, desperate grip. At the intimacy they'd broached, at the strength of their bond, her pulse raced and her emotions soared in a hundred different directions.

There was nothing she could say to ease the pain he'd suffered. And now that it lay before them, there was no way to roll back time, to go back to the carefree day they'd been having—the warmth of the sunshine, the birds chirping overhead, the children laughing...

Jillian hadn't meant to stir up his sorrow when she'd asked about his son, and as a result, she felt somehow to blame for his sadness, for the tears he struggled to hold back. The only thing she could think to do was to thread her fingers through his, tightening their connection.

Clearly, sitting by the playground, watching the happy children and families at play, was just making things worse.

"Come on," she said as she stood and drew him to his feet. "Let's go back to the truck and get the cooler."

They returned to the picnic area in silence, joined together by more than their clasped hands.

She kept the conversation light while they ate lunch, something she continued to do on the drive back to his apartment. Yet even though they'd managed to maintain upbeat subjects, her thoughts were lugged down by the heart-wrenching disclosure.

Shane had said he hadn't taken his son's death very well. Had he fallen apart? Found it difficult to put one foot in front of the other and make it through the day?

That's the way Jillian had felt, after she'd first learned of Thomas's affairs. But there was no comparison. Losing a baby would have been unspeakably worse.

Once they were back at his place, Jillian went through the motions of making dinner. Then they'd topped off the tasty meal—baked chicken, rice pilaf and broccoli—with ice cream sundaes.

On the outside, they'd both forgotten about Joey, about the grief and sadness. But she suspected it was something that would always be buried in Shane's heart, ready to erupt at any time.

After they washed the dishes, he asked, "How about a movie?"

"Good idea."

Twenty minutes later, Jillian and Shane sat on the sofa, watching an action-adventure flick. Jillian had forgotten the name of it, since she didn't normally like much violence. But this one wasn't too bad.

He'd asked her to choose the movie they were going to watch, and she felt that it was only fair to opt for something he might like—something that would get his mind off kids and families.

For a moment, she'd wondered if Shane's move from Houston to Brighton Valley had been some kind of escape for him, too.

Maybe. But it didn't explain him assaulting a suspect in his custody. Though, to be honest, she had yet to see any sign of temper or mean streak in him. Ever since she'd met him, he'd been nothing but sweet and thoughtful.

She tried to focus on the television screen, where bullets continued to fly and ricochet off brick walls, where the good guy was surrounded by the bad guys. When she glanced at Shane, she saw that he had leaned forward, caught up in the tension created by a Hollywood gunfight. But Jillian just couldn't lose herself in the story or the action.

Finally, when things were headed for a showdown

of one kind or another, she stood. "I'm going to take a shower, if you don't mind."

"Now?" he asked. "You'll miss the ending."

She smiled, not at all concerned about that. "I have a feeling it's going to all work out just fine."

And, if luck was in their favor, real life would offer them that same guarantee.

Thirty minutes later, Jillian returned to the living room, wearing a pale blue robe over a white cotton gown. Her hair was wrapped in a towel turban, and her feet were bare.

Shane had been watching a baseball game on ESPN, but he reached for the remote, more interested in the beautiful woman standing before him, the woman who threatened to turn his life inside out. So he lowered the volume and gave her his full attention.

"Are you going to bed now?" he asked.

"I think so." She bit down on her lip, lifted her hand and fingered the lapel of her robe, clearly nervous.

Was she holding something back? Or trying to build up the courage to spit it out?

Instead of pressing her by asking what was on her mind, he waited until she found the words.

"I'm not sure when you plan to turn in tonight," she finally said, "but you don't need to sleep on the couch again. There's plenty of room for you in the bed."

Shane again reached for the remote, this time shutting off the television completely. "Are you sure about that?"

Her cheeks flushed, and a shy smile crept across her

face. "I wasn't talking about sex, but it certainly won't hurt for us to sleep in the same bed."

Shane wouldn't argue with her there, and while he'd be more than willing—in fact, more than eager—to have sex, he counted her concession as progress just the same.

The way he saw it, sleeping together—even if there wasn't any sex involved—meant they might be getting closer to working things out between them.

Was she willing to consider having a relationship with him, after all? One that went beyond coparenting?

"I realize that I was the one who wanted to take things slow and to get to know each other better before we consider dating." She gave a little shrug. "But we took a big step toward intimacy and friendship today, so it seems silly to have you sleep on the couch, all cramped up."

By intimacy, was she talking about him spilling his guts at the park, getting all teary-eyed and laying open his broken heart for her to see?

In the long run, revealing the details of Joey's death had probably been cathartic for him, but it also had shown Jillian a weak and vulnerable side of him that he wasn't proud of having. And one that might have scared off another woman.

Still, he figured they were taking another step in the right direction.

"You don't have to come to bed now," she said. "Your side will be waiting for you whenever you're ready."

He'd rather hear that *she'd* be waiting for him, but

there was no need to press for more at this point. They had twelve more nights together, which meant that there was still plenty of time for a sexual relationship to bloom.

Their lovemaking had been too good for it not to.

"I'm ready to turn in, too," he said. "But I'm going to shower first."

Ten minutes later, Shane entered the bedroom wearing a pair of boxer shorts, even though he usually slept in the raw.

Jillian, who smelled of shampoo, lotion and lilacs, was lying on her side, facing the wall.

Was she asleep? Or only pretending to be?

It was hard to know for sure, but either way, she was tempting as hell. Still, he'd always been able to hold firm when he wanted to, so he climbed into bed, careful not to bounce or jiggle the mattress.

He lay still beside her for the longest time, tempted to reach out to her—with his words or his arms—and deciding not to do either.

But, interestingly enough, when dawn broke over downtown Brighton Valley, bringing a faint light to the bedroom, Shane woke to find himself cuddling Jillian as if their bodies had minds of their own.

They lay spooned together, her back pressing against his chest. One of his arms was under her head, the other lay over her waist.

He'd awakened like this before—in her suite at the hotel. On that morning in early March, he'd slipped out of bed quietly. So now, given a second chance to sleep with her, he had an almost overwhelming urge to wake her with a kiss and a gentle yet eager caress.

Just the thought of drawing her closer to him, pressing his growing erection against her bottom, brought a smile to his face.

As he continued to hold her, relishing her lilac scent, she stretched in his arms, like a waking cat that had been snoozing in the sun. Then she rolled over, facing him. As her eyes opened, as she woke to the reality of where she was and who she was with, her lips parted.

Shane smiled, but he didn't move either his arms or his hands. "How'd you sleep?"

She blinked, and surprise swept across her face, yet she didn't pull away. "I slept okay. How about you?"

He'd certainly woken up a lot better than he'd slept, but he wasn't about to reveal that.

"Much better than the night before last," he said.

She slowly pulled away, as if reluctant to leave his arms.

He wasn't ready to let her go, either, and once again, he fought the urge to give her a blood-stirring, heart pounding kiss.

But he didn't want to push her. Waking up in a lover's embrace would have to be good enough for now.

As the sun stretched high in the East Texas sky, Shane and Jillian drove nearly ten miles outside downtown Brighton Valley to the Walkers' ranch. He was looking forward to showing her the place where he worked, but he also wanted her to meet the couple who had become his close friends.

While traveling along the county road, they passed the Sam Houston Elementary School, Roy's Feed and Grain, and the Flying K Auto Parts Store before reaching open land again.

"How much farther is it?" Jillian asked.

"Just another couple of minutes."

She nodded, then glanced out the passenger window at the passing scenery.

"Like I told you before," Shane said, "Dan and Eva are great people. You'll really like them. Of course, Eva might ask about our plans for the future, but if she does, she'll do it gracefully." He chuckled. "In fact, she'll be so nice about it that you might not even know that you're being quizzed."

Jillian placed a hand on her distended womb and turned to him, her brow furrowed. "It's hard enough talking about the future with *you*. I'm not sure I want to discuss it with anyone else at this point."

"I can understand that. But keep in mind that if Eva asks, it's only because she wants everyone to be as happy as she and Dan are."

Of course, Shane had reason to be skeptical of the whole white-picket-fence dream and to be leery about making the same mistakes all over again. And Jillian certainly did, too.

"Are you sure they're going to be okay with… *things?*" she asked.

"You mean about us staying together in a one-bedroom apartment? Or about you expecting my baby when we're not married?"

She nodded. "And maybe for us having a one-night stand."

"First of all, that night in Houston was incredible. And it fulfilled a need in both of us that went beyond sex. So it wasn't a one-night stand, especially with a baby on the way. And even if it was, it's no one's business but our own." He stole a glance across the seat, saw her nod in agreement. Yet her expression remained pensive.

For a woman who'd once hobnobbed with Houston's high society, she appeared to be more self-conscious than Shane had expected her to be. But then again, maybe it was her experience with that particular social circle that had her so apprehensive now.

"What did those people do to you?" he asked.

Her eyes widened in surprise. "What people?"

"Your ex-husband, his family and friends."

"What makes you think they did something?"

"Because I don't see you as normally self-conscious, but I figure your self-esteem probably took a hard blow when that jerk cheated on you."

She arched a brow. "What makes you think that?"

"I have good instincts when it comes to reading people."

He reached across the seat, took her hand in his, then gave it a gentle squeeze. "Don't worry about what other people think. You're ten times the person most of them are."

"Maybe you're right." Jillian shrugged. "But I'm more to blame than anyone. I got caught up in a fairy tale. And while my life might have appeared to be picture-book-perfect on the outside, it was actually sad and lonely most of the time."

"Do you want to talk about it?" he asked, thinking that he'd actually felt a little better after telling her about Joey.

She seemed to ponder his question for a moment, then eased back into her seat. "Our wedding was really over-the-top—almost fit for royalty. We took a three-week honeymoon in Europe, and Thomas and I moved into a spacious family-owned estate in Houston. I was given carte blanche to decorate the house any way I wanted to, but after that was done, I had very little to do, other than getting dressed up and going to various charity events."

"Were your in-laws good to you?"

"Outwardly, yes. They were very generous. But they were also very controlling and pushy. They interfered more times than not."

Marcia had said the same thing about Shane's family, and for a moment, he wondered how Jillian would feel about the outspoken Hollisters, but he didn't dwell on it.

"So your in-laws created problems in your marriage?"

"I guess you could say that—although indirectly."

"What do you mean?"

"I wanted more out of life than attending social functions, and Thomas couldn't understand that. Instead, he insisted I get involved with his mother's philanthropic projects. And he implied that we'd both be miserable if I didn't yield to her wishes."

"So you gave up your dream for his world."

"More or less." Jillian was quiet for a moment. "I'd always been a good girl who'd never given my grandparents a bit of trouble, so rebellion never came easy for me. And as a wife, I fell into the role Thomas— and his mother—expected of me. And it was a lonely, unfulfilling life. I'd hoped having a baby would be the answer, but after a couple of years trying, I wasn't able to get pregnant."

Shane glanced at her swollen belly, then smiled. "I guess it's safe to say you weren't the one with the fertility problem."

"Apparently not. I'd begged Thomas to go with me to a specialist for testing, but he refused."

"Didn't he want kids?"

"He said he did. But maybe he was afraid to find out that he was infertile. I don't know. Either way, things were always tense when he was around. And when he began to travel on business, I was actually relieved to have him gone."

"Is that when he started messing around?"

"I think so. He was gone more often than not. And then one of his girlfriends called him at home, instead of the office. And…well, his secret was out."

"He was a fool," Shane said.

"Thanks." As she glanced out at the passing scenery, a smile chased away her pensive expression.

"What's so funny?" he asked.

"When I confronted him, I was so angry that I did something completely out of character for me." Her eyes glimmered, and a pair of the cutest dimples formed on her cheeks. "I called him everything but his given name, then threw an expensive vase against the wall, shattering it into a zillion pieces."

"I can't blame you for that." Shane chuckled. "It seems to me that he had that and a whole lot more coming."

Shane understood only too well how emotion could come into play and make someone want to break something—or hit someone. And he wasn't just talking about all of the domestic violence calls he'd gone on, when a cop never knew what to expect.

Shane had lost it once, too. But he wasn't going to tell Jillian that he'd been enraged to the point of striking a perp several times.

Instead, he reached out and took her hand. "You won't meet nicer or more down-to-earth people than the Walkers. So don't worry about impressing them. They're going to like you and accept you—just the way you are."

She gave his hand a squeeze, letting him know she trusted him and making him feel almost heroic. But unwilling to let it go completely to his head, he focused on the road.

As they neared the entrance to the ranch, he pointed to the right and then to the left. "See those cattle grazing in the pastures along both sides of the road?"

"Yes."

"They're part of Dan's spread."

Moments later, they reached the entrance to the ranch, which was marked by a big green mailbox—a plastic replica of a John Deere tractor.

Shane turned in, drove through the open gate and followed the tree-lined driveway until he reached the house and the outbuildings. Then he parked by the barn, next to Dan's white flatbed truck.

He shut off the ignition and turned to Jillian with a smile. "This is it. What do you think so far?"

"It's nice." Jillian scanned the yard, turning to the yellow clapboard house with white trim, where Dan's uncle, the man who'd raised him, sat on the porch in a rocker.

"Who's that?" she asked.

"That's Hank Walker. He can be a little cantankerous at times, but don't let his gruff exterior scare you. He's actually as gentle as a spring lamb."

Before they could open the pickup doors, Jack and Jill, the cattle dogs, ran out of the barn, barking to announce the arrival of guests.

As Shane and Jillian climbed out of the truck, Kaylee and Kevin came out of the barn, following the dogs.

Shane introduced the twins to Jillian, then while she greeted the kids, he gave the dogs each a rub behind the ears.

It had taken him a while to warm up to the Walker twins, but not nearly as long as he'd thought it would. He wasn't sure why that was, but he'd been giving it some thought lately and had come up with an interesting possibility.

Marcia had never met the Walkers, and she'd never blamed them for her unhappiness.

"I've never visited a ranch before," Jillian told Kevin,

"so this is a real treat for me. Thanks for letting me come see it."

"No problem," Kevin said. "We like having company and showing them around. Do you want to ride one of the horses? I can saddle it for you."

Shane stroked the back of the eight-year-old cowboy's head. "Kevin is a good hand with the horses. And he's learning how to rope and cut cattle, too."

"That's really impressive." Jillian rested her hand on top of her pregnant tummy. "And thanks for the offer, but I don't want to ride today. Maybe you can take me out the next time I come to the ranch."

When the front door swung open, two-year-old Sofia stepped out on the porch, followed by her brother Steven. Together they ran toward Shane.

About that time, Hank got to his feet and grabbed his cane. Then he shuffled across the porch, his gait a bit unsteady. As he approached, he reached out an arthritic hand to Jillian. "Shane told us you'd be coming. When's the baby due?"

Jillian blessed the old man with a smile. "December third."

Hank whistled. "Before you know it, this place is going to be bursting at the seams with little ones."

Apparently, he was assuming that Jillian would be a permanent fixture on the ranch, although the jury was still out on that. Either way, Shane didn't correct him.

Hank gave Shane a nudge with his arm. "Did you know Eva's expecting again, too?"

"No, I didn't."

Hank chuckled. "I'm not sure how they're going to

handle another little rug rat around here. The baby will make five. 'Course, they got me to help 'em.''

About that time, Dan and Eva Walker came out of the house, crossed the porch, walked down the steps and approached Shane and Jillian with welcoming smiles. Shane introduced them as his friends, rather than his employers, since they'd become like family to him in the past six months.

"And this is Jillian Wilkes," Shane said, turning to the woman who was pregnant with his child.

Jillian didn't usually like to be the focus of so much attention, but when Dan reached out, she took his hand and gave it a warm shake. He was a ruggedly handsome man with light brown hair and blue eyes. Yet there was a gentleness about him.

"It's nice to meet you," Jillian said, before turning to his wife.

Eva Walker, whose olive complexion and long dark hair suggested she might be Latina, was a beautiful woman, in spite of a rather ugly burn scar that ran from the underside of her chin down to her throat. Yet it was the sincerity in her warm brown eyes that drew Jillian's attention and set her mind at ease.

"We're glad you came," Eva said.

"If you don't mind," Shane told Dan, "I'd like to show Jillian around the ranch."

"Not at all." The rancher slipped his arm around his wife's waist and drew her to his side.

"We'll have lunch when you get back," Eva said.

With that, Shane took Jillian by the hand, and they were off.

After checking out the stalls, the horses and the office, they walked along the outside corral that fenced a couple of mares. Shane explained that they were working horses—trained to cut cattle out of the herd.

Next they continued on to the pasture, following a path that led to the creek.

The sun was especially bright, the temperature warm, the breeze light. And after a tour that took more than an hour, Shane brought Jillian back to the house and into the kitchen, where Eva was making lunch.

She had bread spread upon the countertops, as well as apple slices and oatmeal cookies. And when she spotted Jillian and Shane, she brightened and gave them her full attention—at least until the kids came running.

"Kaylee, will you and Kevin take the little ones into the bathroom and wash up? I'll have your lunch ready in a few minutes."

The older girl nodded, then helped her brother herd the younger twins out of the room.

About that time, Dan opened the back door and entered the mudroom. "Shane, I've got something I'd like you to see. Do you mind coming out to the barn?"

"Sure." Shane turned to Jillian. "I'll be right back."

"Take your time. I'll help make lunch."

Moments later, Eva opened up the fridge and pulled out lunch meat, cheese, mayonnaise, mustard, lettuce and tomatoes. Then she placed them on the countertop.

"You have beautiful children," Jillian said.

"Thanks. Things can get awfully hectic around here, and they can be a lot of work, but I can't imagine my life without them. I'm sure you'll find that to be the case, too." She glanced at Jillian's baby bump, then smiled. "Do you know if you're going to have a girl or a boy?"

"I'd told the doctor I wanted to be surprised when I had my last sonogram, but that's no longer true. I'm really curious now. And since I'd like to set up a nursery, it would be nice to know whether I should focus on trucks and cars or butterflies and kittens."

Before Eva could comment, Kevin dashed into the kitchen. "Mom, can we watch that new SpongeBob movie until lunch is ready?"

"Why don't you watch that Mickey Mouse DVD until I put Sofia and Steven down for a nap. Then you and Kaylee will be able to watch TV without them bothering you."

He seemed to think about her suggestion, then said, "Okay" and dashed out of the room.

Eva reached for the peanut butter and jelly. "I'd better get the little ones fed first."

"I see that there's a lot of careful orchestrating that goes on around here."

Eva grinned. "That's for sure. Dan and I try to stay a step ahead of them whenever we can, but every once in a while, something unexpected happens to really throw us off stride."

"Like what?" Jillian asked.

"Well, a couple of months ago, Kaylee came home from school sick with the intestinal flu." Eva blew out a sigh. "It wasn't more than an hour later when Kevin's stomach began to bother him, too. And by morning, both Sofia and Steven had it."

"That must have been awful. Passing germs around has got to be the downside of having a big family."

Eva chuckled. "You can't believe what that day was like. Dan and I were moving from one sick kid to the next. And when Shane stopped by the house to check on us, he felt so sorry for us that he spent the morning helping us clean up after the kids and doing tons of laundry. He was amazing. And a real blessing."

"I can see how having a second pair of hands would be helpful in a family with two sets of twins."

It was also nice to know Shane had gone above and beyond. And that he hadn't been scared off by sick kids. That had to be a plus, didn't it?

"What can I do to help?" Jillian asked.

"You can peel and slice the apples, if you'd like."

Jillian reached for a knife from the wooden butcher block on the counter, then carried the fruit to the sink. Before turning on the water, she said, "Hank mentioned that you and Dan are expecting again."

Eva smiled, and her eyes brightened. "We haven't made an official announcement yet, but it's true. We hadn't planned on having another child, but I guess God had other ideas."

"You seem happy, though."

"Oh, I am. Babies are a gift, especially the unexpected ones."

Jillian placed a hand on her tummy. Her baby hadn't been planned, either, but she considered her pregnancy a blessing.

Before long, Eva brought the children into the

kitchen for lunch. After wiping sticky fingers, she took the little ones off to bed for a nap.

Kevin and Kaylee went into the living room to watch the DVD they'd been waiting to see, just as the men returned from the barn.

Lunch was pleasant, and so was the conversation. Jillian was glad that she'd met the Walkers. Shane had been right about them. They were nice people, a loving couple and a wonderful family.

As Shane drove her back to Brighton Valley, she reflected upon her time at the ranch. "Thanks for bringing me today. I had a really good time."

"I thought you would."

More than that, Jillian realized that she now had a woman to talk to about pregnancy and babies. Her friend Katie, as sweet as she was, had never been married. So it was nice knowing that she had Eva.

"The Walkers are sure going to have their hands full when the new baby comes," Jillian said. "I can't even imagine what it would be like to have five kids. Wow."

When they arrived back at the apartment, Shane parked in back of the diner. Then they headed for the stairway that led to the rear entrance.

As Jillian made her way up the steps, something pulled low in her belly. Something sharp and painful. She stopped abruptly, gasped and put her hand on her stomach.

"What's the matter?" Shane asked.

"Something hurts."

"What?"

"I don't know." She stood there a moment, stroking low on her belly.

Deciding to continue on, she took two more steps before it happened again. "Whoa."

"Was it a cramp?" he asked. "Or maybe a contraction?"

"I don't know. I've never had a baby before."

They stood in the stairway, not moving up or down.

After a beat—and another painful twinge—Shane clicked his tongue. "That's it. You need to see a doctor."

"But he's in Houston."

"We're not making a two-hour drive for medical advice. I'm taking you to the E.R. at the Brighton Valley Medical Center."

She wanted to argue, to downplay the pain, but the whole baby experience was new to her, and she had to admit she was a little worried herself.

But was this something that required a visit to the emergency room?

"We could go upstairs and wait to see if it goes away," she said.

Shane reached for her waist. "Don't take another step, Jillian. I'm going to carry you down the stairs and put you in the truck."

She wanted to object, to say that she could walk, but as Shane scooped her into his arms, as she caught a whiff of his musky scent, she let down her defenses for the first time since the night they'd met and let the cowboy have his way.

Chapter Nine

Shane drove Jillian straight to the Brighton Valley Medical Center and followed the sign to the emergency room.

"How are you feeling now?" he asked, as he pulled into a parking space.

"I'm okay." She glanced out the window at the white stucco building, then rubbed her belly. "It's feeling a little better now. It's probably nothing."

"Maybe, but it won't hurt to have you checked out by a doctor."

After Shane parked, he slid out from behind the wheel, circled the pickup and opened Jillian's door. Then he took her hand and held it until they entered the E.R. and Jillian was directed to a triage area, where a nurse determined which patients needed to be seen first.

While Jillian explained her pain and the details of her pregnancy, Shane scanned the waiting room, which didn't appear to be especially busy today, thank goodness.

He couldn't count the number of times he'd experienced busy E.R.'s in Houston, when he'd brought a perp or a victim in for treatment. And he knew that some patients waited for hours to be seen.

Shane figured it wouldn't hurt to remind the nurse what was at stake, what could go wrong. "Under the circumstances, since she's pregnant and might be in premature labor, she'll see a doctor right away, won't she?"

"No," the triage nurse said. "We'll be sending her up to the obstetrical floor. They're better equipped to examine and treat her up there. Just give me a minute or two, and we'll have an orderly take her upstairs in a wheelchair."

Shane gave Jillian's hand a gentle squeeze, hoping she felt as relieved as he did at the news.

"In fact," the nurse added, "why don't you take a seat in the waiting room for a few minutes? It won't be long."

After a clerk from the reception desk took Jillian's insurance information, they released her to find a chair with the others who waited with hacking coughs, stomachaches and visible wounds.

It seemed like ages, but was probably only a matter of minutes, before a tall, slender nurse with black spiky hair called Jillian's name. Five minutes later, after an elevator ride and a trip down several corridors, they arrived in the obstetrical unit, where Jillian was assigned to an exam room. After her vitals were taken, she was given a gown and told to undress.

Thinking she would probably want some privacy, Shane said, "I'll wait outside."

He'd hoped she might stop him, which would mean that their friendship—or whatever their relationship was—had made a turn of some kind, growing stronger and more intimate than before. Yet she let him leave.

The nurse followed him out, but they didn't have to wait long. Once Jillian had changed out of her street clothes, he and the nurse returned to the room.

When the two of them were left alone, he asked, "So how are you feeling now?"

"Better. In fact, I'm afraid I might have made a bigger deal out of those pains than I should have."

"Don't worry about that. This is just a precaution."

Moments later, they were introduced to Dr. Selena Ramirez, the resident obstetrician, an attractive woman of average height. She was young—probably only in her late twenties or early thirties, with expressive green eyes and a reassuring smile.

After asking Jillian about the pain she'd had, the doctor had her lie back on the table while she pressed on her stomach to feel the size of her uterus. Then she reached for a pair of gloves, explaining that she would need to give her an internal exam.

"I'll be right outside," Shane said, as he stepped into

the hall again, leaned against the wall and waited next to the door.

Being on an obstetrical floor—the smell, the sound of a newborn's cry, the happy smiles of pregnant women or new mothers walking the halls—caused memories of Marcia's pregnancy to surface.

Shane had been thrilled to learn he was going to be a father. He'd always adored his many nieces and nephews, and had been glad to know that his child would soon be a part of the happy-go-lucky Hollister brood.

He'd also hoped and prayed that having a baby would make his wife happy and more content to stay married. But by the time Joey had taken his first steps, Marcia again asked for a divorce. At that point, Shane had finally been ready to throw in the marital towel, too. The only thing that had torn him up was the fact he wouldn't see his son on a daily basis.

To make matters worse, Marcia met another man and moved to Arizona with him, taking their son with her.

Of course, Shane had objected, but she'd argued that a baby needed its mother, and that he had no right to stop her from being happy. So he'd reluctantly let her go and poured himself into his work, seeing Joey as often as he could.

"Code Blue—Neonatal Nursery."

The overhead announcement of an emergency affecting one of the newborns sent a chill through Shane, along with an unexpected wave of fresh grief.

After Joey's death, as one day stretched into the next, the only thing that had kept him going had been his family and his job. Then, one day, his temper and his grief had gotten the best of him.

He and Sylvia Dominguez, his partner, had been hunting day and night for Lyle Bailey, a suspected child kidnapper who'd killed his latest victim. Knowing the details of the crime had served to make Shane focus on nothing else but prohibiting the perp from hurting another child, destroying another family.

Following a lead, he and his partner had found him holed up in a woodshed behind a house, and when Lyle had tried to run, Shane had tackled him to the ground. He could have held him there, locking on a pair of handcuffs, but for some reason, Shane had snapped and hit the guy a couple of times, something he'd never done before.

It had been the first—and only—time he'd ever felt so out of control.

Bailey's attorney had filed police brutality charges against the department, and Shane was suspended from duty with pay. Internal Affairs finally let him off with a warning. But after that incident, his job no longer helped to keep his mind off his troubles and his grief.

So he'd taken a leave of absence, left town and eventually ended up in Brighton Valley, where he found work on Dan Walker's ranch.

"Code Blue—canceled."

Thank God. He hated to think of any parents having to go through what he'd gone through.

Now here he was, expecting another child and no closer to having the happy family he'd always wanted.

"You can come back now," the nurse said to him from behind the slightly opened door.

When Shane entered the exam room, Dr. Ramirez explained that there was no sign of labor.

"Sometimes, one of the ligaments that holds the uterus in place is pulled. So that's probably what happened today." She turned to Jillian, who was sitting up on the exam table. "Why don't you go home and take it easy tonight. But give me a call if that pain comes back."

Jillian seemed to be okay with both the diagnosis and the instructions, so Shane was, too.

Not that he wasn't still worried about her and the baby.

"There's just one more thing I'd like to do," Dr. Ramirez said. "If you'll lie back on the table, we'll give you a sonogram and double-check to make sure everything is okay on the inside."

Shane was about to excuse himself and leave the room, just as he'd done before, but he wanted to see the baby—*his* baby.

If Jillian had any objections to him staying in the room, she didn't say anything. Instead, she lay down on the exam table.

As the nurse wheeled in a machine, Dr. Ramirez lifted Jillian's gown, then squeezed out a dab of gel and smeared it on her rounded belly.

As the sonogram began, the doctor studied the screen. And so did Shane. Just like the time Marcia had the very same test run, he was intrigued by the image of the growing child in the mother's womb.

"The baby looks good," Dr. Ramirez said. "Strong heartbeat, healthy umbilical cord."

"Can you tell if it's a boy or girl?" Jillian asked.

"It's…" the doctor said, as she zeroed in on the screen, "…a girl."

A *girl*.

As much as Shane had missed Joey, as often as he'd imagined himself coaching a Little League team or taking his son fishing at the lake, the thought of a girl nearly took the breath out of him.

He hadn't wanted to replace Joey. He'd just hoped to recover those paternal feelings, like pride and love. And with the doctor's announcement that it appeared as though his daughter was healthy, all those hopes and dreams came rushing back to him.

Without giving it a thought, he bent down, placed his lips near Jillian's ear and whispered, "Are you okay with us having a girl?"

Jillian looked up at him and smiled. As their gazes met and locked, happy tears overflowed and streamed down her face, convincing him that she wasn't just cool with it, she was over the moon.

"What about you?" she asked. "Are you up to being the daddy of a little girl?"

He smiled, then brushed a kiss on her brow. "Absolutely. As long as she's as pretty as you."

For a moment, everything seemed perfect, and Shane couldn't help thinking that life would be beautiful this time around.

How could it not be?

At least, as long as Jillian agreed to let Shane be involved in his daughter's life.

Once Shane had gotten Jillian home and comfortable, he went downstairs to Caroline's Diner and ordered dinner to go—the pot roast and apple pie that the sign claimed the sheriff had eaten.

Shane had plenty of stuff in the pantry, as well as the refrigerator, to cook for dinner. But he didn't want Jillian to even think about getting up or helping out. She was reclining on the sofa, with her feet up on a stack of pillows, the television remote in her hands.

Now, as he took a seat at an empty table near the front of the diner, he waited for Margie to bring out his order.

He'd been more than relieved to know that Jillian's pain hadn't been an indication of preterm labor and that the baby—a girl, imagine that—appeared to be healthy.

Jillian had mentioned on the way home that she'd really liked Dr. Ramirez. In fact, she thought the Brighton Valley obstetrician had spent more time with her than the doctor she had back in Houston.

Shane wondered if there was any chance she might want to switch obstetricians and stay in town until she delivered. He sure hoped so.

When the front door of the diner opened, he looked up to see Sheriff Jennings enter. He lit up when he spotted Shane, moseyed up to him and reached out his right arm in greeting.

"How's it going?" Shane asked, as the two men shook hands.

"Not bad." Sam folded his arms around his ample belly and grinned. "You're just the guy I wanted to see."

"Oh, yeah? What's up?"

"I told you about my buddy Charlie Boswell, the fire chief who just retired."

"Yes, you mentioned that he was taking his wife on a cruise of some kind."

"He's also been getting in a lot of fishing lately, something I haven't had time to do since last August."

"Sounds like the life to me," Shane said.

"Me, too. In fact, Caroline and I were talking last night, and she asked how I felt about retiring. I'd never expected to turn in my badge, thinking they'd have to pry it from my hands. But I thought about it all night long, and when morning came around, I started to make a list of all the things I'd do if I had a little time off."

"So why'd you want to talk to me?"

"Well, now I'm not saying that I've made up my mind. But if I did decide to give up my position here in town, how would you feel about taking my place— even if it was just in the interim?"

"Until a permanent sheriff could be found?"

Sam nodded. "I'd have to talk to the county commission, but they were impressed with the help you gave me on that burglary case. I'm sure they'd appoint you in a heartbeat."

"I honestly don't know," Shane said. Thing was, if he agreed, even for a while, he'd be leaving Dan in the lurch. And that didn't sit well with him. Besides, he really liked working on the ranch. But there was a part of him that missed police work, and he didn't want to be too quick to decline the offer. "I'd have to think about it, I guess."

"You do that," Sam said, before waving at some people in the rear of the restaurant and heading over to join them, leaving Shane to his thoughts.

If he had reason to believe that Jillian would consider settling in the valley, if there was any future for them together, he'd need to find some kind of job that provided health benefits.

Of course, if she insisted upon living in Houston, he was going to be in a real quandary. Because with each passing day he spent in a small town, he became more and more convinced that he'd never want to return to life in the big city.

But what if Jillian decided Brighton Valley would never be her cup of tea? Where would that leave them?

Right back in the same place he and Marcia had once been. And Shane couldn't figure out what he'd do this time around.

As Jillian climbed from the shower and dried off with one of Shane's white, fluffy towels, she glanced at her image in the mirror. Her tummy seemed to be growing bigger every day, but the baby wasn't anywhere near ready to be born. She was so glad when Dr. Ramirez told her that everything was going well, that the baby wasn't going to come early and that…

I'm going to have a little girl.

Her heart had filled to the brim with love for the child she'd yet to meet, and Shane seemed to be pleased at the news, as well. In fact, he'd been so supportive during yesterday's health scare that it was difficult not to believe that he truly cared about her and the baby.

But was he insisting upon being a part of the baby's life because he hoped their baby would replace the little boy he lost?

She certainly hoped that wasn't the case.

There were other things to consider when it came to contemplating any kind of life together—love for one thing, and loyalty for another.

Sure, a healthy sexual relationship was important—and it wouldn't be a problem for them. But there was more to life than sex.

After slipping on her cotton gown, she went into the living area of Shane's small apartment and waited for him to bring dinner upstairs. While she had the chance, she picked up her cell phone and dialed her grandmother's number.

"Hi, Gram. I just called to say hello."

"I'm so glad you did."

"Are you feeling okay?" Jillian asked, concerned at the hoarse sound of Gram's familiar voice. "It sounds as though you might be coming down with a cold."

"I have a scratchy throat and a bit of a cough, but it's nothing I can't deal with. How are things going? Are you okay? You really don't know that man very well."

"He's a nice guy, Gram. You have nothing to worry about."

There was no need to tell her about the visit to the E.R. today, especially since it had proved to be no big deal.

"Is he treating you well?"

"Shane's been a perfect gentleman." In fact, he'd been...wonderful.

"He hasn't tried to take advantage of you, has he?"

On the contrary. "He's been very sweet and respectful." In fact, he'd been everything Jillian could have hoped for.

"I'm glad to hear that," Gram said. "Since the two of you will be having a child together, it's important that you be friends."

That was true. And little did Gram know, Jillian would be sleeping with that "friend" in an hour or so.

Of course, the doctor had said to take it easy, so there was no chance that they'd end up having sex tonight. But would they eventually become lovers again while she was staying with him?

Just the thought sent a delicious shiver that pooled low and warm in the depths of her.

It was still too soon to tell if they would pick up where they'd left off, she supposed—even though it would be incredibly easy to succumb to temptation.

Maybe she should make an extra effort to stay strong. Their relationship as friends and coparents was going to be difficult enough, especially with them living two hours away from each other. Trying to be sometimes lovers, too...?

That might be too much to handle.

Would Shane consider moving back to Houston? If so, could something permanent work out between them?

"When will you be coming home?" Gram asked,

her graveled voice reminding Jillian that she might be sicker than she'd let on.

"I'd planned to stay two weeks, which is right before my next appointment with Dr. Allan." Jillian had been looking forward to that appointment, since she wanted to make sure the baby was healthy, that her pregnancy was going well. But she'd just had confirmation from Dr. Ramirez that the baby—her *daughter*—was growing as expected, that all seemed to be fine.

For a moment, she wanted to share the news with Gram. But that would mean she'd have to admit to having that pain earlier today, and Jillian didn't want to worry her any more than necessary.

"I assume you asked Dr. Allan for permission to travel," Gram said.

"Yes, he was fine with it."

Dr. Allan was one of many doctors in a large and prestigious obstetrical group in Houston, although Jillian sometimes got the feeling that his practice was too big, that he was too busy and rushed her appointments.

Dr. Ramirez, on the other hand, had been both thorough and reassuring. Maybe it was because she was a woman herself and was more nurturing by nature. It was hard to say.

Gram coughed into the phone, then apologized.

"I don't like the sound of that cough," Jillian said. "Have you called the doctor?"

"Not yet."

As heavy, booted footsteps thumped on the stairway outside, Jillian realized Shane had returned with dinner.

"Listen, Gram. I have to go. But promise me you'll

see the doctor if you're not feeling better in the morning. And that you'll call me, either way."

"I will, honey. Don't worry about me."

It was hard not to. Gram had not only raised Jillian, but she was the only family she had left.

After the line disconnected, she set her cell phone on the lamp table, then met Shane at the door. As he scanned the length of her, his gaze zeroed in on her breasts.

Oops. The thin cotton fabric of her white cotton gown was probably a little more see-through than she'd realized.

As his gaze lifted and met hers, a shot of awareness rushed through her. For a moment, she was tempted to let her hormones take the lead, but it was the maternal hormones that kicked into play and insisted she heed them.

What if having sex caused that pain to return? What if Dr. Ramirez was wrong about it being something minor?

So in spite of wishing things were different, she tried to put a platonic spin on things.

"So what did the sheriff eat tonight?" she asked.

"Pot roast with all the fixings and apple pie."

As Shane set out the food on the table, he asked, "How do you feel about going for a little drive tomorrow?"

"Where?"

"I thought I'd take you to Wexler. There's a store that sells baby stuff. And since we know the baby's going to be a girl, I thought it might be fun to check things out."

Jillian hadn't planned to purchase anything until she got back to Houston, since it wouldn't do her any good to buy things in Brighton Valley and haul them home—or have them shipped. But it might be nice to see what was available and to get some decorating ideas.

"Sure, that sounds like fun." As she started for the table, where he'd set out their meal, he looked up, his gaze again sketching over her.

With the light behind her, she suspected that he was taking in every curve of her body, from her breasts, to her hips, to her belly. And while she really ought to be a little concerned by the raw hunger in his eyes, she felt a sense of feminine power, too.

Of course, as heady as that was and as tempted as she was to make love to him again and experience all the passion she'd felt in his arms, that wasn't going to do her any good this evening, when she was determined to follow the doctor's orders about taking it easy.

Of course, Dr. Ramirez hadn't said anything about being careful tomorrow morning.

And by the way her body seemed to gravitate toward his while they slept, she had a feeling that it was only a matter of time when they'd wake to find temptation too strong to ignore.

Chapter Ten

Although Shane's bed was plenty big enough for two, Jillian woke up the next morning on his side of the king-size mattress, her left arm draped over his shoulder, her leg entwined with his.

Yesterday, when they'd shut off the TV and turned in for the night, she'd purposely faced the wall. But for some reason, by the time morning rolled around, their bodies had seemed to find each other.

At least, her body had sought out his.

She probably ought to move before he opened his eyes and realized that she'd somehow crept from her side to his, but it felt so natural to lie with him, so good to snuggle up against him.

It seemed as though they hadn't slept together in ages, even though it had only been the night before.

And she tried to figure out why it felt as though such a long time had passed.

The connection they seemed to share? The healing she'd found in his embrace?

Meeting Shane last March had been the first step in getting over the effects of her divorce and restoring her confidence as a woman, something Thomas's infidelity had sent reeling. And now that she and Shane had come together again, now that they were developing a…

What? A friendship?

As she lay stretched along the length of him, her body pressed against his and taking comfort in his warmth, his strength, his presence, it seemed as though there was more than friendship going on here, although she was reluctant to admit just what it was.

The scare she'd had yesterday, even though it had proved to be unfounded, and the trip to the E.R. had bonded them in an unexpected way. And the sonogram that had revealed their baby growing in the womb, their *daughter,* had locked them into their roles as parents.

Was there even more going on than that?

As Shane began to stir, Jillian wanted nothing more than to caress his cheek, to trail her fingers along the morning stubble on his jaw that gave him a roughened edge. To watch his eyes open and know that his very first vision upon waking would be her. But that was a little too risky at this point, a little too…*married.*

Still, whatever it was that she was feeling for him, including the physical attraction that she'd never been able to shake, was too tender and new to analyze. But one thing was clear. She didn't want to risk falling heart over head for him yet, even though she had to admit that the possibility of that happening was growing by leaps and bounds.

It was too soon for her to forget that he'd assaulted a suspect he'd taken into custody.

Of course, he'd been nothing but sweet and kind and gentle to her since she'd arrived in Brighton Valley. But that didn't mean he didn't have a temper, that it wasn't lurking somewhere, under the surface and ready to snap.

His breathing changed, and he moved, reaching for her hand. Then he brought it to his lips and pressed a kiss into her palm, sending a tremor of heat to her feminine core.

Had a move so simple, so sweet, been such a turn-on before?

"Good morning," he said, his voice still laden with sleep. "How are you feeling?"

Hot. Aroused. And maybe even willing to see where this morning takes us.

Before she could deal with the temptation, the urge to throw caution to the wind and come up with a response, he asked, "No more of those pains?"

Now she could answer in all honesty. "None whatsoever."

"That's good to hear." He turned slightly, so that his back was on the mattress, and he turned his head to allow his eyes to meet hers.

She appreciated his concern for her, for the baby. Bracing herself up on an elbow, she rose up and offered him a good-morning smile. "How'd you sleep?"

"Great." When he lobbed her a crooked grin, she no longer seemed to care whether he had a temper or a short fuse.

Instead, she was tempted to skim her fingers along his chest. To brush her thumbs across his nipples, knowing—*remembering*—how he reacted to that particular stimulation. But before she could lift her hand and place it on his chest, he rolled to the side and climbed out of bed, leaving her in a pool of disappointment.

"Do you want to use the bathroom first?" he asked.

No, she wanted to stay in bed, to experiment with the thoughts and feelings that had been playing on her mind since waking this morning. And while she'd assumed he'd sense where her thoughts were heading, it was clear that he wasn't a mind reader.

For that, she supposed she should be grateful, since her head was urging one thing and her body another.

"No," she told him, "I can wait. Go ahead."

Maybe he planned to come back to bed as soon as he was done, and when he did—that is, *if* he did—she'd...

Well, she wasn't exactly sure what she'd do. But she doubted that he'd put up an argument over anything she might suggest.

He yawned and stretched, flexing muscles in his chest and forearms she'd discovered in Houston and had nearly forgotten about.

"What time do you want to go into Wexler?" he asked.

Seriously? He was ready to start the day and wasn't planning to return to bed?

Again, she tried to tell herself that she should be grateful, that it was too soon for the ideas she'd been having. Yet the strangest sense of disappointment settled over her.

"I don't care," she said. "It's up to you."

"Then let's shower, have a quick breakfast and get out of here. I'm actually looking forward to seeing the kind of stuff they have at that store for baby girls."

To be honest, so was Jillian. But she couldn't help thinking that he seemed to be more excited about the baby than he was in having Jillian in his bed.

And for a moment, she felt both abandoned and rejected.

As Shane headed for the bathroom, leaving her to deal with the confusing emotions, she tried to shake them off, telling herself that she should be happy that he was looking forward to their child's birth. That her pregnancy hadn't made him uneasy about what the future might bring.

But now Jillian had something else to worry about, something about Shane's past that gave her pause.

If he saw the baby as some kind of replacement for the one he'd lost, then maybe Jillian was merely a means to the end for him....

As Shane drove Jillian into Wexler to check out The Baby Corral, a store that sold furniture, clothing and other items new parents might need, he couldn't help noting how quiet she'd been this morning—unusually so.

It might have been only his imagination, he supposed. But something seemed to have her in deep thought, and not knowing what was bothering her left him a little unbalanced, since there was so much riding on her plans for the future.

As his marriage to Marcia had begun to unravel, the two of them had grown more and more introspective, so to see Jillian doing the same thing was a little disconcerting.

Earlier, when he'd woken up wrapped in her arms, he'd been tempted to kiss her, to run his hands along her hips, to venture into a little morning foreplay. And while he'd noted a spark of passion in her eyes, in her smile, he'd decided only an insensitive jerk would suggest a romp in bed when the doctor had told her to take it easy the day before.

So he'd headed for the shower before she could see how primed and ready he was for sex.

When he went to the kitchen to put on a pot of coffee and whip up some scrambled eggs, she'd gone into the bathroom. It seemed as though she'd stayed in there for hours, and when she came out, as pretty as any woman he'd ever seen, her makeup just right and every hair in place, he'd tried to coax a smile out of her.

But all she'd been able to muster was a makeshift grin, which hadn't been what he'd expected, what he'd wanted. And that's when he'd realized something was off.

So even now, as they entered Wexler city limits and he turned down the main drag, she still hadn't opened up.

"Are you sure you're feeling okay?" he asked, hoping

that a shopping trip wasn't going to be too taxing and wishing he hadn't suggested it.

"I'm fine." She'd offered him another smile which didn't quite reach her eyes.

Shane couldn't see pursuing it any further, so he focused on the road until they reached the store.

After he parked in front, they headed to the door. Once inside the trendy baby shop, she seemed to brighten at the variety offered.

"Let's check out the cribs and dressers," he said, as he led her to the back of the store.

"All right."

They took time to check out the various furniture styles, as well as the colorful comforters and matching mobiles that would entertain the baby while she was small. Jillian seemed to favor one with teddy bears, each one sporting a different-colored bow tie.

"Do you see anything you like?" he asked, thinking he'd buy it for her—although maybe not today.

"This one is nice." She touched one of the spindles of a light oak crib.

As they continued through the store and they passed a display of bottles and nipples, he asked, "Do you plan to nurse?"

"Yes, I'd like to." She turned to him and offered a shy smile, which made him decide the quiet spell might be over. "I know that December seems like a long time off, but it's getting closer every day, especially after seeing the baby on that sonogram screen yesterday."

"I know what you mean." The baby had sure become real to him over the past twenty-four hours. And her due date would be here before they knew it. In fact, for the first time since Joey died, he found himself looking forward to Christmas and all that it brought…stockings on the mantel, presents under the tree. A new baby…

As they continued down one aisle and up another, he decided to throw out an idea he'd been tossing around, just to see what she would say.

"Would you consider sticking around in Brighton Valley a little longer? After all, you mentioned that you might postpone your student teaching until next term. And you said that you liked Dr. Ramirez. If there was a problem, you'd be in good hands."

As she turned to him, a swath of confusion crossed her face. "You want me to extend my visit?"

"Why not?" He certainly found the idea appealing. "I've been thinking about getting a bigger place anyway, so if the quarters are too tight for you, that won't be an issue for long."

"I…" She tilted her head slightly, as though the movement might help her wrap her mind around his suggestion. "But my doctor is in Houston."

"You said you weren't all that impressed with him."

"Actually, Dr. Allan has a great reputation and a degree from one of the top medical schools in the country. It's just that he's so busy, I sometimes feel as though my appointments are cut short." She continued down the aisle, just as pensive as ever, then she stopped and faced him. "I really like Dr. Ramirez and wouldn't mind having her deliver the baby. But it's really not feasible for me to stay in Brighton Valley."

"Why not?"

"Because my life is in Houston, Shane."

He'd figured as much, and even though he'd expected that to be her answer, it still left an ache in his chest, a twist in his gut.

As they reached a display of rocking chairs, she stopped by one in particular and took a seat. Then, as she set the chair in motion, she looked up at him and smiled—one that lit her eyes this time. "I really like this one."

"Good. Let's get it."

"Today?"

"Sure, why not?"

"Because I've been trying to conserve my money. And while I plan to buy some things new, I figured I could pick up some furniture, like a rocker, at a consignment store in Houston."

"I was offering to buy *that* rocker—as a gift."

"You don't need to do that."

"I want to."

She didn't object any more, yet she continued to sit, to sway back and forth. Then she caught his gaze again. "Can I ask you a question?"

"Sure."

"Do you miss working as a cop? Do you think you'll ever go back?"

"I miss parts of it," he admitted. "I was good at what I did. But in the last year or so, I've found small-town life to be a lot more appealing than living in the city."

"You don't miss the excitement?"

"Sure, sometimes." There was an adrenaline rush that came with pursuing and arresting a suspect, of knowing that he'd gotten a dangerous perp off the streets. But Shane wasn't sure if Jillian would understand the complexities of his job, of missing it, yet not wanting to go back.

Marcia certainly wouldn't have.

"I was ready for a change in my life," he said. "And working on Dan's ranch and living in Brighton Valley suits me right now."

He couldn't really explain why that was the case when a part of him did miss the excitement, the thrill and the knowledge that he'd made the streets a little safer. But here in Brighton Valley, he seemed to have shaken the bad memories, the reminders of why his marriage had fallen apart and how he'd come to lose Joey.

Out here, where the Texas sky seemed bluer, the air cleaner, the sun brighter and warmer, he'd found a sense of peace that he doubted he'd ever be able to find in the city. So going back to Houston wasn't in his immediate plans—if ever.

He'd hoped that Jillian would find something comforting about small-town life, too. But that didn't appear to be happening. And if it didn't, it was going to make it a real challenge—if not completely impossible—to work out a way to coparent and share custody of their daughter.

He supposed he'd have to at least consider moving back to Houston, but that meant he'd be forced to make a life choice that didn't appeal to him, all because a woman he cared about wasn't willing to find a compromise they could both deal with—like splitting the distance and making a commute work.

Yet even if he gave up his happiness for hers, there was still no guarantee that things would turn out the way he wanted them to.

But how did he want it to turn out?

He wanted to be a part of his child's life. That was for sure. But what about Jillian?

His feelings for her went beyond the fact that they'd conceived a child together and that they would be involved with each other one way or another for the next eighteen years or longer. He still wasn't sure just how far those feelings went, but he'd go so far as to say that he'd like for them to be lovers again.

"Uh-oh." Jillian's rocker came to a halt.

Damn. Had her pain come back? Had Dr. Ramirez been wrong when she'd said there probably wasn't anything to worry about?

"What's the matter?" Shane asked.

Jillian hadn't meant to gasp—or to forget that she hadn't talked to Gram yet today. So she said, "I'm sorry. My grandmother wasn't feeling well last night, and she promised to call me this morning and let me know how she was doing, but she hasn't."

She glanced at her wristwatch, noting that it was nearly noon, so she reached into her purse and pulled out her cell. Then she dialed her grandmother's number.

As she waited for Gram to answer, Shane took a seat in the rocker next to hers.

Again, Jillian couldn't help thinking about how supportive he'd been, how understanding. Yet was his kindness a result of his concern for her—or for the baby?

About the time Jillian was ready to hang up and call one of the elderly woman's neighbors, Gram answered, her voice almost a bark.

"You forgot to call me. How are you feeling?"

"I'm not feeling any better. And my cough might be worse. I have a call in to the doctor, and I'm waiting to hear from him."

"How's your throat? It sounds as though it still hurts."

"It does, but don't worry about me. I'm sure it's just a cold."

How could Jillian not worry? Gram was a widow in her mid-seventies, and she didn't need any more health issues than the ones she already had: diabetes, high blood pressure and high cholesterol.

"I was hoping the doctor would phone in a prescription to the pharmacy," Gram said. "I really don't want to drive to his office. I don't have much energy."

What about driving to the pharmacy?

Jillian clucked her tongue. She couldn't help thinking that she ought to head back to Houston and make sure Gram got to her doctor's office, as well as to the pharmacy, to pick up any prescriptions she might need.

"I'm going to come home. I can be there by two o'clock or a little after, so when the doctor does call, try to set up an appointment in the late afternoon."

"You don't need to cut your visit short. I can call Margie, my neighbor, if I need a ride. Or I can drive myself. I really don't want to be a bother to anyone."

"You're not a bother," Jillian said. "And this isn't up for negotiation. I'm coming home."

After ending the call, Jillian looked at Shane, saw him watching her intently.

"What's the matter?" he asked.

"I need to take my grandmother to see the doctor. She's getting older, and I'm all she has."

"I understand. Why don't I drive you?"

As tempting as his offer was, as much as she'd like for him to meet the woman who'd raised her—and maybe get a second opinion about his character—she slowly shook her head. After all, she'd nearly jumped his bones this morning, and he hadn't seemed the least bit interested.

He might have made it clear that he wanted to be a part of his child's life, but he hadn't said anything about the importance of being a part of hers.

Besides, he didn't want to live in Houston, and because of Gram, that's where Jillian needed to be. She couldn't very well jump in the car and make a two-hour drive every time her grandmother needed something.

As if that wasn't reason enough, the university was located there. And Jillian was more apt to find a good job or a teaching position in the city.

She'd already given up her dreams, as well as her independence, for a man once. There was no way she'd do that again.

No, she had to remain in Houston. And the sooner Shane realized that, the better.

"Thanks for the offer," she told him, "but I'd rather take my own car and drive myself."

His eyes narrowed a bit, as if he wasn't at all pleased by her decision. Or was he finally revealing a bit of the darkness or anger that might lie under his surface, ready to break free?

Shane shifted his weight, glanced down at his feet, then back to her, shuttering any shadow she might have detected just seconds ago.

"Okay," he said, "then let's go. I'll take you to the apartment to get your things and your car."

"Thanks, I appreciate that."

But he didn't comment further. Instead, he led her out of the store, leaving the rocker and anything else he'd planned to purchase for the baby behind.

The ride back to Shane's apartment was a quiet one. But what was there to say?

Jillian was leaving and unlikely to return. He'd hoped that she would have enjoyed staying with him, that she would have liked small-town life, that she might eventually consider moving in with him over the fall and becoming a family.

But apparently, that wasn't going to happen.

While Shane wanted to stop her from packing her things and leaving permanently, to insist she give him a shot to prove he could be a good father, he clamped his mouth shut.

He wasn't about to be put into the same no-win position that he'd been in with Marcia. And he even went so far as to wonder if walking away now might be easier to distance himself—before he had a chance to bond with the baby, before he had a chance to see more than a grainy, black-and-white image of his little girl. Maybe then it wouldn't hurt as badly as it had when Marcia had taken Joey away.

He'd been backed into corners before, when he'd been faced with two choices—one was bad, the other was worse. And this was clearly one of them.

After parking the truck behind Caroline's Diner, Shane walked behind Jillian as she climbed the stairs and entered the small apartment that had once seemed like home.

He waited while she packed her bags, then carried them out to her car for her.

"Thanks so much for having me," she said.

"No problem. I'm glad you had a chance to see Brighton Valley and to get to know me a little better."

She went up on tiptoe, placed her hand on his cheek, then planted a sweet, it-was-nice-while-it-lasted kiss on his lips.

It took all he had not to wrap his arms around her and pull her close, kissing her senseless in one last attempt to keep her here—or to encourage her to return.

But the memories of the past—of the fights he'd had with Marcia over his family interference, his job and Joey—everything that was important to him—came pummeling down on him, and he took a step back, letting her go.

Jillian had never met his family, but he remembered the conversation they'd had on the way home from the ranch, when they'd talked about the Walkers expecting a new baby.

Eva's going to have her hands full, Jillian had said.

I can't even imagine what it would be like to have five kids. Wow.

If she couldn't imagine herself having a big family, how could she ever accept the boisterous Hollister clan?

Marcia certainly hadn't dealt very well with all of Shane's siblings, their spouses and the twelve-at-last-count nieces and nephews. Hell, even Shane had distanced himself from them—although he wasn't sure why.

Because Marcia had accused them of being outspoken and intrusive, he supposed, and to avoid trouble at home, he'd tried to cut the cord. But even that hadn't worked.

So why did he avoid being around them now?

He wasn't sure. Guilt maybe—for staying away so long.

What had they ever done to hurt him—at least, intentionally?

He wondered if she'd feel any differently about them than Marcia had—and hoped she would.

"Did your ex come from a big family?" he asked.

She shook her head. "And thank goodness for that. Dealing with his mother was tough enough as it was."

He remembered her saying the woman was controlling. Interfering.

"Well, I'd better go," Jillian said. "Thanks again."

"Keep in touch."

"I will." Then she climbed into her car.

As much as Shane might have hoped that Jillian would be open to meeting his family, he was beginning to realize that he'd only be opening a can of worms to introduce them. And as he watched her drive away, he came to the sad conclusion that he'd probably been right all along.

Their relationship had been doomed from day one.

Chapter Eleven

Although Jillian had been gone only a few days, Shane missed her more than he'd ever thought possible. But he'd be damned if he would chase after her like a love-sick puppy.

He'd called her a couple of hours after she'd left, just to make sure that she'd gotten home safely, then again later that evening, to ask about her grandmother's condition.

"She has pneumonia and is in the hospital," Jillian had told him, "but the doctor assured us that she was only being admitted as a precaution. He expects her to respond to antibiotics, and as soon as she does, she'll be discharged."

"Then it was good that you went home," he said, in spite of his disappointment that she'd ended her visit early and his belief that she probably wouldn't come back—even if she could.

"You're right. I really had no choice. My grand-mother had hoped to get by with only a prescription and no office visit, so I'm glad I insisted upon taking her in."

At that point, Shane could have asked Jillian to come back to Brighton Valley after her grandmother was feeling better, but why bother? She'd clammed up that morning, before she'd even made the call to the older woman, so something else had been bothering her. Something she hadn't wanted to share with him.

Shane had chased after a woman before, and it hadn't done him a bit of good. So he wasn't about to do it again.

When they'd said their goodbyes and ended the phone call, he'd turned on the TV, hoping to shut Jillian out of his mind. But it hadn't done the trick. When he'd finally turned in for the night and slipped between the sheets, her lilac scent teased him, until his bed had never felt so empty. Not even after Marcia had left him, which had come as a bit of a surprise.

The next day, he'd gone back to the ranch, hoping that some hard work would help him get his life back on track.

Dan had asked why he'd come back before the week was up, but all Shane had said was that there'd been a family emergency, and Jillian had to return home.

Now it was the weekend—Sunday morning to be precise. And without having any physical labor to ease his mind, he'd decided to drive into Houston to see his parents, who typically barbecued on weekend afternoons for anyone who cared to show up.

They'd be surprised to see him, since he lived so far away and had used the distance as an excuse more often than not. But it was finally time for him to stop avoiding the family get-togethers and join the Hollister fold once again.

He hadn't planned to drop in on Jillian, even though he'd been tempted to give her a call every five minutes on his two-hour drive to the city. So much for keeping her out of his mind. Who was he fooling?

Now look at him. In spite of his best efforts to leave well enough alone, he found himself heading for her apartment rather than to his parents' house.

After parking in one of the visitor spaces, he made his way to her front door and rang the bell. When she answered and spotted him on the porch, her bluebonnet eyes widened and her lips parted.

He'd been envisioning her for days on end, remembering her lilac scent and her pretty smile, yet he hadn't realized the actual sight of her would steal the breath right out of him.

"What a surprise," she said.

He grinned. "I was in the area and thought I'd stop by."

She stepped aside to let him into the small living room.

"How's your grandmother doing?" he asked.

"Much better. She only stayed in the hospital overnight, then I brought her here to stay with me for a couple of days. I took her home this morning. She wanted to water her plants and check on things."

"I'm glad she's feeling better."

"Me, too."

He waited an awkward beat, then said, "I hope you don't mind me stopping by."

"No, not at all. Why don't you have a seat?"

He scanned the room, deciding upon the sofa. "Thanks."

"Why did you have to come to Houston?" she asked, as she sat, too, and rested one hand in her lap, the other on her pregnant tummy.

"My folks live in the Woodlands," he explained, "just off Arbolitos Drive. And since they've been complaining that they don't see me often enough, I decided it was time to pay them a visit."

"That's nice."

Nice? That's it? As much as Shane had wanted to see her, to hear her voice, he'd hoped to get more than that out of her. But as the initial awkwardness stretched between them, he wasn't sure what to say, what to do.

He probably ought to make an excuse and leave, but decided to give it one more shot. And since he was going to lay his heart on the line once—and *only* once—he decided to level with her about his feelings and ask what she wanted from him.

"You know that I plan to be a part of the baby's life, which means I'll be a part of yours, too."

"I know." She offered him a smile. "You can't very well be one or the other, can you?"

Yeah, he supposed that was true.

"I want you to know that I wouldn't be opposed to getting married."

Her smile faded, although he couldn't blame her for being a little surprised by a semiproposal like that. So he added, "Not right away, of course. We'd have to work through things, but I see a future for us as a couple."

She crossed her arms, as though bracing herself. Or distancing herself. Hell if he knew.

Should he have mentioned anything about love?

Women were funny about things like that. But how could he profess to loving her when he wasn't all that sure about the depth of his feelings himself? And even if he was, he wasn't sure he could admit to something like that without hearing it come from her first. Throwing those three little words out there would really put him behind the emotional eight ball.

So why wasn't she saying anything?

Damn, he was botching this all up. He'd never been comfortable talking about feelings, not to his family or to Marcia, when the two of them had been married. So what made him think he'd learned to open up about that stuff now, when there was so much riding upon him and Jillian working out some kind of relationship?

"I really care about you, Shane. And I think you'll make a good father. So I'm okay with you being a part of the baby's life, but marriage is…well, it's a big step. I just got divorced. I'm not ready for that kind of commitment, not yet." She tucked a strand of hair behind her ear.

Shane wanted to object, although he wasn't sure why.

Jillian clearly wasn't interested in marriage or a future together. And, apparently, being his lover again was out, too. Otherwise, she wouldn't have put him off each time they'd taken a step in that direction.

But there was one thing he would take a stand on, without giving a damn whether he was compromising himself or not. And that was being a father to their baby.

"For what it's worth," Jillian said, "I'm still trying to prove to myself that I don't need a man to rescue me, even if that means going without and struggling financially. It's important for me to know that I can support myself and my daughter."

"She's my daughter, too."

"I realize that."

Did she really? Then why did she think she had to call all the shots?

The past, it seemed, was repeating itself. And Shane wasn't about to go through that frustration all over again. So he glanced at his wristwatch, then got to his feet. There wasn't any reason for him to stay. He'd offered marriage—well, at least he'd brought it up as a possibility—and Jillian had pretty much thrown it right back in his face.

He wasn't going to beat a dead horse, at least when it came to Jillian. On the other hand, he wouldn't give up his child without a fight.

"Are you leaving?" she asked.

"Yeah, I need to go." But not because anyone at his parents' house was expecting him. Right now, his heart

was knotting up inside because of all he stood to lose—
and he wasn't just talking about his daughter.

He'd fallen for Jillian. As much as he'd like to dis-
pute the possibility, he couldn't. Not here. Not now.

As he walked to the door, she followed him. But he
let himself out.

Then he headed for his pickup without looking back.

As Jillian watched Shane climb into his truck, she
wanted to call him back, to tell him that they had more
to talk about. But fear caused her tongue to freeze and
her feet to root to the floor.

After she and Thomas had split, she'd been determined to protect herself from getting involved in
another bad relationship—and the pain and disappointment that went with it. So she'd resisted Shane and her
growing attraction to him.

So how's that working for you? a small voice asked.

To be honest? Not so well. Her heart ached at the
thought of losing him for good, and she wasn't sure
how to make things right. Was it too late to even try?

She had to admit that she'd handled things badly
when he'd stopped by, but his surprise visit had thrown
her off balance, and so had his mention of marriage.

Yet somewhere, deep in her heart, she'd hoped
that they could have become a couple someday—
and a family. But Shane hadn't said anything about
love, and there was no way Jillian would ever consider
making a lifetime commitment without that one critical
ingredient.

So she closed the front door, locking herself into her apartment.

Yet instead of gaining the sense of security she'd been expecting, a cold, lonely chill settled within her, leaving her feeling lost and more alone than ever before.

For nearly twenty minutes, she continued to struggle with her emotions, as well as her plans for the future, but she was still no closer to a resolution.

Jillian could certainly use a friend right now, but Katie, her old college roommate, wasn't going to fit the bill this time. She didn't just want to chat and vent; she needed some guidance from someone who loved her unconditionally.

So she picked up the telephone and called the one person in the world she could always depend upon for level-headed advice.

When Gram answered, Jillian gripped the receiver as though she could reinforce their connection, strengthening it.

"I've got a problem," she told the older woman.

"What's the matter?"

In the past, while talking to Gram about the night she'd met Shane and invited him back to her room, Jillian had held back a lot of details, but she wouldn't do that now. If she wanted her grandmother's advice, she would have to lay it all on the table, letting the older woman know just what the problem was—and how it was tearing her apart.

So Jillian told her grandmother everything—about the romantic dinner they'd had, the arousing kiss they'd shared on the dance floor and the fact that Shane had turned her broken heart on end, jump-starting the healing process and making her feel like a desirable woman again.

She didn't go into the specifics of their lovemaking, of course, but she did admit that they'd been sexually compatible.

Compatible? that small voice asked. How about downright *combustible?*

There was no disputing that, but she did her best to shake off the heated memories. Then she mentioned that Shane's young son had died. She also shared what she'd read about his assault of the suspect who'd been in his custody, the resulting suspension from the force and, of course, his reinstatement after a thorough investigation. She ended by telling Gram that he'd ultimately left the HPD altogether.

Jillian even went so far as to admit that Thomas had been abusive at times, although he'd never gone so far as to strike her. And her concern that Shane might have a short fuse or a violent streak, too.

"Has he given you any reason to believe that about him?" Gram asked.

"Honestly? None at all."

Gram seemed to ponder that response for a moment, then asked, "When did he lose his child? Was it before or after the incident with that suspect?"

"His son died first, I think. Why?"

"Because that time in his life must have been filled with grief."

"I'm sure it was."

"When he snapped with that suspect, he might have

been in a bad place emotionally. And if that's the case, then maybe you should cut him a little slack, honey."

Jillian hadn't thought about that, even after that day at the park when he'd told her about Joey's death. For some reason, she hadn't put the two incidences together, and she probably should have.

Either way, how could she make an assumption about Shane's character without even asking him what had happened that day? Or to consider the reasons that may have led up to it?

"Thanks for talking to me, Gram. You've given me a lot to think about."

"I haven't met that young man, Jilly, but I trust your judgment. And it's time that you started to trust yourself again, too."

After saying goodbye and ending the call, Jillian sat back on the sofa.

Gram had been widowed after losing the love of her life, so it wasn't any wonder that she had a romantic streak, that she believed marriages and relationships could go the distance, even though Jillian's personal experience suggested otherwise.

As hope began to rear its head, Jillian couldn't help thinking—and *believing*—that the older woman might be right.

Had she made a big mistake by letting Shane leave before telling him how she felt—even if she wasn't entirely sure?

She could have told him how much she'd appreciated all the little things he'd done to make her visit in

Brighton Valley special—and enjoyable. Having him with her in the E.R. that day had been comforting, too.

As she thought about the sonogram, about her and Shane watching their baby move within the womb, she remembered his excitement, his support.

And in spite of her fear that he considered their baby a replacement for the son he'd lost, she realized that he'd seemed pleased to learn that their child was a girl.

He'd even been willing to get a bigger place to live and to purchase a brand-new rocking chair for her to put in the nursery she planned to create.

As Jillian took it all in, she blew out a sigh. Why hadn't she realized that there was far more to Shane Hollister than met the eye, although what met the eye was enough to set her heart soaring and her hormones pumping?

In fact, even though she'd been dragging her feet about getting physically involved with him, she liked sleeping with him and waking in his arms. She even wanted to make love to him again.

And again.

Did all of that mean that she could fall in love with him?

Or maybe she already had.

So now what? she wondered.

The urge to talk to him grew until she had no choice but to act upon it.

He was probably already at his parents' house by now, with his family. Maybe she should call him, discuss her thoughts and feelings over the phone. But a face-to-face conversation would be best.

My folks live in the Woodlands...just off Arbolitos Drive.

Jillian didn't know exactly which house belonged to Mr. and Mrs. Hollister, but she could certainly find the street. And then she could drive up one side and down the other until she spotted Shane's pickup.

There would probably be a party in progress, but she wasn't going to let that stop her. She was going to walk right up to the front door—baby bump and all. Then she would ring the bell and ask to speak to Shane.

He hadn't said much about his family, and she wasn't sure why he hadn't. So she wasn't sure what his family would think of her showing up unannounced, unwed and pregnant. But she didn't care. She needed to talk to Shane and make things right.

She just hoped it wasn't too late.

After climbing into his pickup and leaving Jillian's house, Shane had sworn under his breath, ashamed of himself for practically groveling.

Right then and there, he'd been tempted to head back to Brighton Valley, with its clear blue skies and wide-open spaces, where he'd created a new life for himself.

Instead, he drove across town to the Woodlands, turned onto Arbolitos Drive and proceeded until he arrived at his folks' house.

There were a couple of cars parked in front already, as well as two of his nephews playing catch on the lawn. He sat in his truck for a moment or two, watching his brother John's sons.

The boys were getting bigger, Shane noted. It was

nice to see the oldest coaching the youngest. John must be really proud of them.

Deciding he'd sat in the truck long enough, he climbed out of the driver's seat and headed for the house. As he made his way up the sidewalk, he stopped long enough to say hello to the boys and to add, "Good arm, Trevor."

"Thanks, Uncle Shane. You want to play with us?"

"Maybe later. I have to check in with your grandma first, or I'll be in big trouble." Then he made his way to the front door and let himself in.

He'd barely entered the living room when his sister Mary-Lynn spotted him.

"Hey, Mom," she called. "Come quick. Look what the cat drug in." Then she wrapped Shane in a hug, which he held on to for a beat or two longer than necessary.

For some reason, it felt especially good to have a physical connection with another human being, especially since Jillian had sent him on his way earlier. Not that she'd asked him to leave, but she hadn't done anything to convince him to stay.

"You're certainly a sight for sore eyes," Mary-Lynn told him, as they stepped apart. "You really should come around more often. We miss you."

"I missed you, too." And at that very moment, as the words rolled off his tongue without any conscious thought, he realized they were true.

"So what's new around here?" Shane asked his sister, knowing that she was the go-to girl when it came to learning the scoop about the comings and goings in the family.

"Well, let's see… Colleen's setting a wedding date—November tenth. And Andy will be heading for Camp Pendleton soon, although I'm not sure when."

Before Shane could question whether their baby sister was old enough and wise enough to tie the knot, or whether Andy should have considered another branch of the military, his mother entered the room and clapped her hands.

"Shane! I've been hoping and praying that you'd surprise us one Sunday and come home." Then she wrapped her arms around him in a mama-bear hug, letting him know just how glad she was to see him.

After the welcome-back embrace ended, his mom and his sister headed back to the kitchen, just as Jack, his oldest brother, came into the house from the backyard.

"It's good to see you, little brother."

"Same here."

"So what's new?" Jack asked.

Nothing Shane was ready to talk about yet. So he said, "Not much."

"Are you dating anyone special yet?"

"Nope. I'm too busy riding fence and mucking stalls for that."

"Sounds like a crappy job, if you ask me. If I were you, I'd much rather be chasing after the bad guys—and dating the ladies." Jack, who loved his work with the police department, nodded toward the sliding door that led out to the patio. "Come on outside. I'll buy you a beer and let you know what's been going on at the HPD."

As Shane followed his brother out to the yard, he thought about the dating question and his lack of honesty.

Of course, he and Jillian weren't what you'd call an item. In fact, after today, they weren't really anything—other than coparents, he supposed.

He'd been a fool to stop by her place earlier, and he'd been an even bigger fool to mention marriage or to hint at them having a life together.

From day one, he'd known that a permanent relationship with Jillian wasn't in the cards—even if he'd wished otherwise.

Jack handed Shane a can of beer, and they made small talk for a while. A few minutes later, their father, who'd been napping, joined them outside. They greeted each other, then talked about the scuttlebutt down at the precinct.

As Shane scanned the yard, watching the kids play tag and the adults crack jokes, listening to the bursts of laughter and the escalating voices, he realized that it would take a special woman to appreciate a Hollister get-together.

Marcia certainly hadn't been able to. And Jillian, who was an only child, too, didn't seem able to handle it, either.

Besides that, Jillian had also experienced the best that life could offer when she'd been married, so how could she ever live happily in a blue-collar world?

She'd be miserable. And Shane would find himself back in that same marital turmoil he'd been in before.

No way would he ever want to live like that again.

"You ready for another beer?" Jack asked, as he dipped his hand into the ice chest.

"No, I'm good for now." Shane turned back to the game of tag that his nieces were playing on the grass.

"Shane?" his mom called out.

"Yeah?" He turned to face the sliding door, where his mother stood.

He assumed that she wanted him to do her a favor, like carry something heavy outside or reach a bowl in the top shelf of the cupboard.

Instead, she said, "You have company."

"Me?" He wondered who knew that he'd be here today, since he hadn't told anyone in the family that he was going to show up.

"Yes, *you,*" she said.

"Who is it?" he asked.

"That's what *I'd* like to know." His mother crossed her arms and raised her brow. "She's a beautiful blonde who's obviously pregnant. And she's asking for you."

"Uh-oh," Jack said. "Sounds like you might have been doing a little more than riding fence and mucking stalls while you were in Brighton Valley."

Shane might have had some kind of snappy retort if he hadn't been floored by the news that Jillian was here. And it had to be her. Who else did he know who was blond, beautiful and pregnant?

Trouble was, when he went inside the house and headed for the front door, everyone else seemed to follow him like a string of ducklings.

Chapter Twelve

Jillian stood on the Hollisters' front porch, waiting for Shane's mother to call him to the door.

She'd been invited inside, but until she had a chance to talk to him and he issued the invitation himself, she thought it would be best if she waited here.

But when footsteps sounded—a lot of them—she glanced past the entryway and into the living room, where Shane strode toward her, several of his family members following behind.

Certainly she wouldn't have to tell him what she'd come to say in front of an audience, would she?

He wore a slightly bewildered expression, although she had no idea what her own looked like—uneasy? Embarrassed? Contrite? Maybe a little bit of each?

Still, as he approached, she managed a smile. "I…

uh...need to talk to you." She glanced beyond him—at Mrs. Hollister, as well as a man who could be his brother, and several children.

Shane peeked over his shoulder, at the curious on-lookers, then back to her. "Do you want to take a walk around the block?"

"Sure."

"It might be the only chance we have at some privacy." Then he turned to his mother and said, "Don't wait for me to get back. Go ahead and eat whenever those steaks are done."

Then he stepped onto the porch and closed the door behind him, shutting out the audience.

They started down the sidewalk to the curb, then proceeded down the shady, tree-lined street.

"How'd you know where my parents live?" he asked.

"You told me the neighborhood, as well as the street. I took a drive, then looked for your truck. Actually, I knocked at one of the neighbor's houses by mistake, and a lady told me to go next door."

The sun had risen high overhead, and a breeze ruffled the leaves in the trees, as they continued a casual walk.

"I hope you don't mind that I came by," she said.

"No, that's fine."

"It's just that I wanted to apologize to you—in person."

He pondered her comment for a half beat. "About what?"

"For not being completely open with you about the way I feel. For holding back and for not trusting you."

His steps slowed, and hers did, too. As he turned to face her, as their gazes met and locked, she braced herself for what she'd driven across town to say.

"I think you'll make a wonderful father for our baby. And I'll be happy to share custody with you. But I plan to nurse her, and so... Well, you can understand why I wouldn't want you to take her away from me or keep her overnight."

"I never planned to do that. At least, not when she's little. That's one reason why I..." He glanced down at his boots, shifted his weight, then looked back up again. "I guess that's why I suggested that we work something out, where we could... Well, eventually where we could raise her together."

"You mean move into the same house?" she asked. He'd mentioned marriage, so that's what he must have been thinking.

"I'm willing. But if you're not ready or even interested, I understand."

"It's not that." She cleared her throat, hoping to cut through the complicated feelings she was struggling with, then pressed on with the honesty he deserved. "I enjoyed my time at your place in Brighton Valley. You were a perfect gentleman and... Well, you seem to be too good to be true, and that scares me."

"Why?"

"Because I'm afraid of getting hurt again."

"I can understand that."

"Can you? Because I can't. And it doesn't seem fair to you. I mean, my ex-husband was a lying jerk. And

I've been holding you at bay because I'm afraid that you might not be the man I want you to be."

Shane reached out, caught a strand of her hair, letting it slip through his fingers as though it were spun gold. "You scare me, too. I had a lousy marriage, and my wife never could appreciate my family or my job. Hell, most of the time, she didn't even appreciate *me*. So now I find myself involved with a woman who lives in a world two hours from mine, and she's having our baby."

"So how can we work this out?" she asked.

"Are you willing to compromise?"

"That's what I came here to tell you. I should have said something earlier, but my fears got in the way, even though you've given me nothing to be afraid of."

"Are you saying you'd consider marrying me?" Shane asked. "Maybe someday?"

"That's the problem." She bit her lip, then sought his gaze, his understanding. "Marriage is hard enough when people love each other."

"And you don't think you could ever love me?"

She tilted her head slightly. "I *do* love you, Shane. I'm not sure when it happened—maybe that night at the hotel. All I know is that my feelings for you continue to grow, and I don't know what to do, other than face them head on."

She *loved* him? Shane couldn't believe his ears. He wasn't the only one wrestling with those feelings, with that mind-spinning attraction.

He reached out and cupped her beautiful face, skimming his thumbs across her cheeks, breathing in her lilac scent, basking in her presence. "You have no idea how happy I am to hear that, Jillian, because I love you, too."

"You do?"

He nodded. "I was afraid you wouldn't be able to accept me and the lifestyle I wanted to provide for you. But if we love each other, maybe we can come up with a compromise that will work out without either of us having to give up our dreams."

"I'd like that. And while I wasn't sure how this conversation was going to turn out, I did some thinking about possible solutions on my drive across town."

"So what'd you come up with?"

"Since school is out, and the baby is due in December, there's no reason for me to be in Houston, other than my grandmother. And maybe, if I tell her I'm moving to Brighton Valley and taking the baby with me, she'll consider relocating."

"No kidding?" Shane had hoped she'd feel that way, yet it had all seemed too much of a stretch.

"I'd have to make some phone calls, but I might be able to do my student teaching at the new high school in Brighton Valley—or even the old one in Wexler."

If she was willing to compromise, to go to that extreme for them to be together, then he'd do the same for her. "If it doesn't pan out, if you can't get the position, then I'll do whatever I have to do—even if it means moving back to Houston or taking a desk job. I want us all to be together—as a family."

"It just might work out," she said. "I'd have some

meetings and classes I'd have to attend at the university sometimes, but not every day. So I can probably commute."

"I know it'll work out," he said. "One way or another. We'll find a way."

Then he lowered his mouth to hers, sealing the commitment they intended to make with a kiss that began sweet and precious, then deepened into something soul stirring and filled with promise.

When they came up for air, he drew her tight, amazed at his good fortune.

"I don't know when I've ever been so happy," he said.

"Neither do I."

"I don't know about you," he said, "but Christmas came early this year."

"Speaking of Christmas..." She broke into a radiant smile. "There's going to be three of us by then. Can you believe it? We'll be writing letters for Santa and leaving cookies under the tree before you know it."

Shane thought of Joey, of the first Christmas after his birth. And while the memory was bittersweet, it wasn't nearly as painful as it might have been—before he'd met Jillian and had realized that time really did heal, that life went on.

"I can't wait," he said. "Come on, let's go back to the house and tell my family. We won't have to stay long, but I'd like them to know. I think it'll make them happy."

"All right."

He reached for her hand, then she gave it a tug. "Wait a minute. I have something I want to confess."

"What's that?"

"After I found out I was pregnant, I looked you up on the internet. I was curious and wanted to know more about you."

"I can understand that. I actually did some checking of my own." He gave her hand a gentle squeeze, knowing what she'd probably learned and ready to deal with it now. After all, with her in his corner, he could handle anything. "So what did you find out?"

"An online newspaper account reported the trouble you had with the police department. At the time I read the article, I wondered if you had a violent side. But the more I got to know you, the more I realized you weren't the kind to snap like that. Not unless provoked."

He couldn't blame her for being concerned. And he was glad that she'd come to the conclusion that she and the baby would always be safe with him.

"You don't have to tell me what happened that day if you don't want to. It doesn't matter to me anymore. But I want it to be out in the open, since I want us to always have an open relationship."

He remained silent for a while, rewinding that scene and watching it all over again as it played out in his mind. Then he let it go, wanting the honesty, too.

"His name was Lyle Bailey. And he brutally murdered a little boy. My partner and I had been looking for him, and when we found him, he ran. I took chase, knowing that there'd be no way in hell I'd let him get away. No way I'd let him hurt another child again, ruin another family. And when I caught him... Well, I snapped. All I could see were two little boys in small caskets, the boy he'd murdered and Joey."

Jillian reached up and cupped his cheek, then she drew his lips to hers, kissing him softly, sharing his grief. "I understand."

"I don't have a temper," he explained. "Although I've got to admit that I'm not sure what I would have done to that guy if my partner hadn't stopped me."

It seemed like a dark and horrible thing to share, yet because of the intimacy and honesty that stretched between them, it was the perfect time to set it out there.

"I was suspended, with pay," he added. "You probably read that, too."

"Yes, and I also know that they reinstated you."

His lips pressed together, and he nodded. "But after that, after I assaulted Bailey, I thought it would be a good idea to take a leave of absence to wait until Joey's death wasn't so fresh on my mind."

"Do you ever want to go back to work as a cop?"

"Would it bother you if I did?"

"No, I'm going to support you in whatever you want to do."

Shane couldn't believe his good fortune. How lucky he'd been when he'd spotted Jillian in that bar, when he'd gone back to her hotel room. And he couldn't wait to start their life together, to get ready for their Christmas baby.

"Come on," he said, taking her by the hand. "I need to introduce you to my family before they come looking for us. They might get a little loud and boisterous.

And they'll be full of questions. But if you can handle it for a little while I'll follow you back to your place, where we can be alone."

And where they could seal their love with more than a kiss.

"I hope they like me," she said.

Shane reached for her hand, giving it a gentle squeeze as they headed back to his parents' house. "Don't worry about that. They're going to love you. I'm more concerned about you liking them."

"Why? What's wrong with them?"

"They can be a little quirky at times. And intrusive. And generous and loving, too. You know what I mean?"

"I think so."

As they reached the house, he spotted movement near the shutters, realizing that someone had been peering into the street.

So as he opened the door for Jillian he said, "Okay, you guys. The gig's up. No need to be snoopy, we have an announcement to make."

His mother swept into the room as though she'd just now become aware of their return, although Shane had a feeling she'd been the one doing the peeking out the window.

"This lovely woman is Jillian Wilkes," he said, "and she's expecting my baby—a little girl. We're going to get married, although we haven't decided when."

As the family closed in on them, their smiles revealing their happiness and their willingness to welcome Jillian into the Hollister fold, Shane's heart filled with love—for her, for their child and for the family that only wanted him to be happy.

Jillian opened the door to her small apartment and let Shane inside. She wasn't sure why he'd felt so uneasy about her meeting his family. Sure, they were a little loud and outspoken, but their love for each other was apparent and seemed to spill over into everything they did or said.

They'd ended up staying nearly an hour, since Jillian had felt so welcome and had wanted to join them for dinner.

Now they were back at her apartment, where she scanned the small living area, realizing that this place was only a temporary abode. She had no idea where she and Shane would end up living, but she knew that as long as they were together, anywhere would feel like home.

"Did you get enough to eat?" he asked.

She laughed. "More than enough. Your mom and sisters kept offering me seconds."

Shane slipped behind her and wrapped his arms around her waist. "They mean well."

"I know they do." Jillian turned to face him and stepped into his warm embrace. "But there's something you need to keep in mind."

"What's that?"

"I'm not anything like Marcia. And while I've never had brothers or sisters of my own, I'm actually looking forward to being a part of the Hollister clan—even if they're a little quirky or become intrusive at times."

Shane kissed her, and as her lips parted, as their tongues began to mate, she drew him close, relishing all she'd found in his arms, in his heart.

Somehow, some way, this was all going to work out beautifully.

As she threaded her fingers in his hair, she leaned into him, relishing the feel of his mouth on hers, wanting more. Needing more.

Would she ever get enough of *him*—the man she loved? The man who offered her everything she'd always wanted in life—a family, a home?

As the kiss intensified, as the physical hunger that always simmered between them kicked into high gear, she reached for his belt buckle, letting him know she was ready for more than just a kiss, that she wanted a replay of the first night they'd met.

He followed her lead, undoing his jeans and tugging at his shirttails.

This was what they'd been waiting for since that night in March, when two lonely people met and set about to heal each other.

She reached for his hand and led him to the bedroom, where she began to undress, removing her light jacket and letting it flutter to the ground, unzipping her slacks, pushing the fabric over her hips.

As Jillian shimmied out of her pants, Shane stood transfixed, caught up in an arousal of epic proportions and mesmerized by the provocative way she removed her clothes.

When she stood before him in a pair of lacy white panties and a matching bra, the swell of her pregnancy added a sweet innocence he hadn't quiet expected. He swallowed hard as the woman he loved bared herself to him, offering herself as a gift he would cherish the rest of his life.

With his heart pounding in both love and need, he eased before her, slowly. Reverently. "You're beautiful."

"So are you." She unbuttoned his shirt, sliding the fabric off his shoulders. Then she skimmed her fingers across his chest, sending a shiver through his nerve endings and a shimmy of heat through his blood.

As he removed his shirt completely, he watched as she reached behind her back and unhooked her bra, releasing her breasts. He bent and took a nipple in his mouth, tasting, suckling, taunting until she gasped in pleasure.

Then he scooped her into his arms and laid her on top of the white goose down comforter, where they began to work the magic that had been sparking between them ever since the first time they'd spotted each other at El Jardin, the upscale bar in Houston.

Then, after removing the rest of his clothes, Shane climbed beside her on the bed, never missing a beat, as they picked up right where they'd left off.

When their breathing grew ragged, when they were unable to wait any longer, he entered her, giving her everything he had, loving her fully—with his body, heart and soul.

As they reached an incredible peak, as she gripped his shoulders and cried out with her release, he let go, too, riding the waves of an amazing climax.

When it was over, they continued to hold each other,

basking in their love and in the amazing chemistry they shared. Finally, Shane rolled to the side, taking Jillian with him. As they faced each other, drawing sated smiles, she placed her hand on his chest, over his heart.

"I can hardly believe this," she said, "but making love with you was even more amazing than I remembered."

"I was just thinking the same thing." As he ran his hand along the slope of her hip, a slow smile stretched across his face. "And the best part about it is the fact that it's only going to get better."

She knew he was right, although it was hard to imagine how they could improve perfection. She brushed a hank of hair from his forehead, amazed at the depth of her love for him.

Somehow, it seemed as though they'd always been meant for each other.

"It's too bad we didn't meet each other before we fell into bad first marriages," he said.

"I'm not so sure about that. Maybe all those struggles we dealt with before made us into the people we are today, people who can fully appreciate and love each other."

"Maybe so, honey. But I promise you this. I'm in this for the duration."

"So am I."

With that, he kissed her one more time, with everything he had, everything he was, everything he ever hoped to be.

Epilogue

Three weeks after Jillian and Shane brought Mary Rose Hollister home to their four-bedroom tract house in Brighton Valley, they hosted the family Christmas party as a way to welcome their new daughter into the Hollister fold and to show off their new digs.

Outside, while storm clouds gathered overhead, a December breeze stirred the dried leaves still on the trees. Yet inside, the flames of a small fire in the hearth cast its warmth throughout the living room.

A Christmas tree with blinking white lights and colorful ornaments stood near the bay window that looked out into the street, while the faint scent of pine mingled with the aroma of a turkey baking in the oven.

Along the mantel, adorned with small boughs of pine and a nativity scene, hung three handmade stockings, each filled with goodies that Santa had brought the night before.

Jillian's grandmother, who'd decided to move into the apartment over Carolyn's Diner after Shane and Jillian had found a larger place, was seated on the new rocking chair near the fireplace. As Gram held the eight-pound baby girl, who'd been dressed in a red-and-white sleeper, she marveled over the tufts of dark hair and blue eyes.

"I swear to goodness," Gram said, "Mary Rose is the most beautiful baby I've ever seen."

Jillian thought her daughter was adorable, too, although she and Gram were probably just a wee bit biased.

"Honey?" Shane called, as he came in from the backyard. "Did Jack get here yet? He called a while back, and I gave him directions."

"Not yet," she said. "Do you think he's lost?"

"Maybe not. But he should have gotten here by now."

Dan and Eva Walker had been the first to arrive, along with both sets of twins and Catherine Loza, a friend of theirs who'd been living in Manhattan.

According to what Eva had told Jillian earlier, Catherine had gone through a recent breakup and had wanted to get away. Jillian didn't know the details—and she wouldn't ask—but she couldn't imagine a better place than Brighton Valley to heal a broken heart and to get one's life back on track.

She'd come to love this town and looked forward to starting her student-teaching at Washington High

School in Wexler when the winter semester began in mid-January.

Shane, who'd been appointed sheriff when Sam Jennings retired, was happy with the position, saying that it allowed him the best of both worlds.

When the doorbell chimed, Shane announced, "I'll get it. That's got to be Jack."

All of the Hollisters would be arriving within the next twenty minutes or so, but Jack had started out sooner than the others. And Jillian couldn't wait to see them. Shane's family had been wonderfully supportive, accepting her as a new daughter-in-law and going so far as to include Gram in all of their family gatherings.

Jillian wasn't sure who was happier to hold the family Christmas dinner—her or Shane. They'd been decorating and planning the meal since Thanksgiving.

"Come in," Shane told his brother, who entered along with his wife and two sons.

"Trevor," Shane said to the oldest boy, "why don't you take Evan out to the backyard? The Walkers are back there, checking out the swing set that came with the house."

As the Hollister boys dashed outside, Jillian met Shane at the door to welcome her brother-in-law and his wife. "Thanks for agreeing to have Christmas in Brighton Valley this year. I know it's a long drive for you."

"We wouldn't have missed it," Cindy Hollister said. "Now, where's the baby? I can't wait to hold her. They grow up so fast."

As Jillian pointed to Gram, Jack scanned the living room and said, "Nice house."

"Thanks." Shane slipped his arm around Jillian and pulled her close. "We like it."

And they truly did. Their new home might be miniscule in comparison to the estate in which Jillian had once lived with Thomas, but it resonated with the love and laughter she'd been longing for during those sad, lonely years.

As Jack and his wife followed the kids out to the backyard, Shane drew Jillian into a warm embrace. "Thank you for making this Christmas my best ever."

"I'm the one who should be thanking you."

Then she kissed her husband with all the love in her heart.

* * * * *

HEART & HOME

Heartwarming romances where love can
happen right when you least expect it.

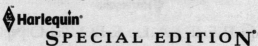

COMING NEXT MONTH
AVAILABLE DECEMBER 27, 2011

You can find more information on upcoming Harlequin® titles,
free excerpts and more at www.HarlequinInsideRomance.com.

HSECNM1211

REQUEST YOUR FREE BOOKS!

2 FREE NOVELS PLUS 2 FREE GIFTS!

◆ Harlequin®

SPECIAL EDITION

Life, Love & Family

YES! Please send me 2 FREE Harlequin® Special Edition novels and my 2 FREE gifts (gifts are worth about $10). After receiving them, if I don't wish to receive any more books, I can return the shipping statement marked "cancel." If I don't cancel, I will receive 6 brand-new novels every month and be billed just $4.49 per book in the U.S. or $5.24 per book in Canada. That's a saving of at least 14% off the cover price! It's quite a bargain! Shipping and handling is just 50¢ per book in the U.S. and 75¢ per book in Canada.* I understand that accepting the 2 free books and gifts places me under no obligation to buy anything. I can always return a shipment and cancel at any time. Even if I never buy another book, the two free books and gifts are mine to keep forever.

235/335 HDN FEGF

Name _____
(PLEASE PRINT)

Address _____ Apt. # _____

City _____ State/Prov. _____ Zip/Postal Code _____

Signature (if under 18, a parent or guardian must sign)

Mail to the Reader Service:
IN U.S.A.: P.O. Box 1867, Buffalo, NY 14240-1867
IN CANADA: P.O. Box 609, Fort Erie, Ontario L2A 5X3

Not valid for current subscribers to Harlequin Special Edition books.

Want to try two free books from another line?
Call 1-800-873-8635 or visit www.ReaderService.com.

* Terms and prices subject to change without notice. Prices do not include applicable taxes. Sales tax applicable in N.Y. Canadian residents will be charged applicable taxes. Offer not valid in Quebec. This offer is limited to one order per household. All orders subject to credit approval. Credit or debit balances in a customer's account(s) may be offset by any other outstanding balance owed by or to the customer. Please allow 4 to 6 weeks for delivery. Offer available while quantities last.

Your Privacy—The Reader Service is committed to protecting your privacy. Our Privacy Policy is available online at www.ReaderService.com or upon request from the Reader Service.

We make a portion of our mailing list available to reputable third parties that offer products we believe may interest you. If you prefer that we not exchange your name with third parties, or if you wish to clarify or modify your communication preferences, please visit us at www.ReaderService.com/consumerschoice or write to us at Reader Service Preference Service, P.O. Box 9062, Buffalo, NY 14269. Include your complete name and address.

HSE11B

SPECIAL EDITION

Life, Love and Family

Karen Templeton

introduces

The FORTUNES *of* TEXAS: Whirlwind Romance

When a tornado destroys Red Rock, Texas,
Christina Hastings finds herself trapped in the
rubble with telecommunications heir
Scott Fortune. He's handsome, smart and
everything Christina has learned to guard herself
against. As they await rescue, an unlikely attraction
forms between the two and Scott soon finds
himself wanting to know about this mysterious
beauty. But can he catch Christina before she runs
away from her true feelings?

FORTUNE'S CINDERELLA

Available December 27th wherever books are sold!

Brittany Grayson survived a horrible ordeal at the hands
of a serial killer known as The Professional…
who's after her now?

Harlequin® Romantic Suspense presents a new installment
in Carla Cassidy's reader-favorite miniseries,
LAWMEN OF BLACK ROCK.

Enjoy a sneak peek of
TOOL BELT DEFENDER.

Available January 2012
from Harlequin® Romantic Suspense.

"**B**rittany?" His voice was deep and pleasant and made her realize she'd been staring at him openmouthed through the screen door.

"Yes, I'm Brittany and you must be…" Her mind suddenly went blank.

"Alex. Alex Crawford, Chad's friend. You called him about a deck?"

As she unlocked the screen, she realized she wasn't quite ready yet to allow a stranger inside, especially a male stranger.

"Yes, I did. It's nice to meet you, Alex. Let's walk around back and I'll show you what I have in mind," she said. She frowned as she realized there was no car in her driveway. "Did you walk here?" she asked.

His eyes were a warm blue that stood out against his tanned face and was complemented by his slightly shaggy dark hair. "I live three doors up." He pointed up the street to the Walker home that had been on the market for a while.

"How long have you lived there?"

"I moved in about six weeks ago," he replied as they

walked around the side of the house.

That explained why she didn't know the Walkers had moved out and Mr. Hard Body had moved in. Six weeks ago she'd still been living at her brother Benjamin's house trying to heal from the trauma she'd lived through.

As they reached the backyard she motioned toward the broken brick patio just outside the back door. "What I'd like is a wooden deck big enough to hold a barbecue pit and an umbrella table and, of course, lots of people."

He nodded and pulled a tape measure from his tool belt. "An outdoor entertainment area," he said.

"Exactly," she replied and watched as he began to walk the site. The last thing Brittany had wanted to think about over the past eight months of her life was men. But looking at Alex Crawford definitely gave her a slight flutter of pure feminine pleasure.

Will Brittany be able to heal in the arms of Alex, her hotter-than-sin handyman...or will a second psychopath silence her forever? Find out in
TOOL BELT DEFENDER
Available January 2012
from Harlequin® Romantic Suspense
wherever books are sold.

Love Inspired® SUSPENSE

RIVETING INSPIRATIONAL ROMANCE

A surprising inheritance takes Caroline Tully to Mississippi to visit her newfound grandfather's home during the holidays. Adopted as a child, she doesn't realize her biological mother's family can't be trusted. When attempts are made on her life, Caroline turns to Donovan Cavanaugh—the only man she can trust—to help catch her would-be killer.

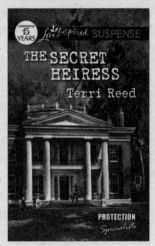

THE SECRET HEIRESS
by Terri Reed

PROTECTION
Specialists

USA TODAY BESTSELLING AUTHOR

DELORES FOSSEN

CONTINUES HER THRILLING MINISERIES

When the unthinkable happens and children are stolen
from a local day care, old rivals Lieutenant Nate Ryland
and Darcy Burkhart team up to find their kids.
Danger lurks at every turn, but will Nate and Darcy
be able to catch the kidnappers before
the kidnappers catch them?

NATE
Find out this January!

Harlequin Presents®

USA TODAY bestselling author

Penny Jordan

brings you her newest romance

PASSION
AND THE PRINCE

Prince Marco di Lucchesi can't hide his proud
disdain for fiery English rose Lily Wrightington—
or his attraction to her! While touring the palazzos
of northern Italy, the atmosphere heats up…until
shadows from Lily's past come out….

*Can Marco keep his passion under wraps
enough to protect her, or will it unleash itself, too?*

Find out in January 2012!